THE KING OF COMEDY
Jeremy STRONG

JAIL BREAK!

Illustrated by Rowan Clifford

PUFFIN

PUFFIN BOOKS

UK | USA | Canada | Ireland | Australia
India | New Zealand | South Africa

Puffin Books is part of the Penguin Random House group of companies
whose addresses can be found at global.penguinrandomhouse.com.

puffinbooks.com

First published 2016
001

Text copyright © Jeremy Strong, 2016
Illustrations copyright © Rowan Clifford, 2016

The moral right of the author and illustrator has been asserted

Set in Baskerville MT
Printed in Great Britain by Clays Ltd, St Ives plc

A CIP catalogue record for this book is available from the British Library

ISBN: 978–0–141–36141–3

MIX
Paper from
responsible sources
FSC® C018179

Penguin Random House is committed to a
sustainable future for our business, our readers
and our planet. This book is made from Forest
Stewardship Council® certified paper.

This is dedicated, at least

financially, to Mastercard

Contents

Introduction

Kraaark! It's me, Croakbag, otherwise known as *Corvus maximus intelligentissimus.* Is that some kind of raven, I hear you ask? You did ask, didn't you? Of course you did, because you're curious. Good. It's very important to be curious and Find Things Out. So make sure you stick your beak into everything. What's that? You haven't got a beak? Well, stick your nose in instead.

I am indeed a raven and a very clever one at that because ravens are the brainiest of all birds. Oh yes. *Corvus biggus brainia.* That's Latin, that is, which is what we Romans speak. *Corvus* means 'raven' in Latin. You can work out what the rest means for yourself. See? Easy! What a brainbox

you are! I can see we shall get along very well. I might even share a biscuit with you or even, if you're very fortunate and I get to like you A LOT, a dead squirrel. They're my favourite. Oh yes! **Kraaark!**

Now then, we've got some catching up to do, so let me fill you in. There's this family I look after, right? They think I'm their pet. Ha ha! Am I in a cage? No. Can I fly about wherever and whenever I like? Yes. So forget the pet thingy. I'm Croakbag the raven. Get over it!

Anyhow, the family. There's Krysis (Father or rather *Pater* in Latin) and Flavia (*Mater*). They've got two children: their daughter Hysteria (fourteen) and a son, Perilus (eleven). Hysteria is in floods of tears (again) because she's got a crush on the brilliant, handsome young charioteer

Scorcha, but – how about this – Scorcha has just
been thrown in prison. Perilus is worried sick
because he pretended to be Scorcha and took
his place in a chariot race and won. That was
all very exciting, but now the chariot team, who
think he's Scorcha, expect him to race again
and Perilus is afraid he'll be found out and then
there'll be TROUBLE.

BUT (and it's a big but, which is why I put it in capital letters like that) there's an EVEN BIGGER PROBLEM. Are you still with me? Good. I knew I'd like you the moment you started reading my story. Go on, have another biscuit. I shan't mind, as long as it's only one. If you want to find out for yourself all the extraordinary things that happened earlier, you'll have to read *Romans on the Rampage!* That was my first book and it's totally amazing, even if I say so myself.

Anyhow, back to the EVEN BIGGER PROBLEM. Krysis has a Very Important Job in Rome. He's head of the Imperial Mint. Now then, take it easy! That doesn't mean he's the Chief Peppermint and is covered in chocolate. The Mint is a serious bit of business. It's the place where all those coins in your pocket are actually made, millions of them – silver, gold! Imagine all that money! Every country has a Mint.

The only thing is a lot of dosh has been disappearing from the Imperial Mint and Krysis's hair is falling out with worry because he doesn't know what's happened to it. He could be in MEGA BAD BOOKS with the Emperor!

So here we go: you're in for a fast and bumpy ride, just like one of those chariots Scorcha likes racing about in. Read on and bring some biscuits with you! **Kraaarkk!**

1. Some Money Goes Missing

Crump crump crump crump!

What on earth was that noise? It was the sound of feet marching up the road, that's what. Krysis stared at his wife, wild-eyed. Flavia stared back at him, even wilder-eyed.

'They're coming!' wailed Krysis, while Flavia dived beneath a table and pulled her *stola* over her head. (*Stola* – it's a big shawl-scarfy kind of thing.)

Upstairs, Perilus was leaning out of his window, watching the soldiers marching along.

'Left, right, left, right!' he shouted down at them, but immediately shut up and turned white when they stopped at the door of the villa and began hammering on it with the handles of their swords.

'Open up!' yelled their leader. 'We are the Imperial Guard, sent by the Emperor himself. Open up at once or we'll, um, we'll, um –' He paused and looked at his men for inspiration. 'What shall we do?' he whispered.

'Kill them?' suggested one.

'Tell them to go to their bedroom and stay there with no supper?' said another.

'Go home?' said the tallest one hopefully.

'No.' Their leader shook his head, frowned and then perked up. 'I know!' He turned back to the door and rapped on it again.

'Open up,' he cried, 'or we'll DO SOMETHING!' He grinned back at his men. 'See,' he told them. 'That'll scare 'em. They won't know what to expect. That will really rattle their cage.'

Inside the villa, Krysis was definitely very rattled. In fact, he was rattling even more than a chariot with one wheel missing. He was desperately trying to squeeze himself under the table too, not to mention pulling Flavia's *stola* over his head at the same time. Meanwhile, one of their slaves, Flippus Floppus, strolled to the front door and opened it.

'Yes?' he enquired.

The leader of the Guard eyed Flippus Floppus from top to toe and back again. 'Are you Krysis, Chief Peppermint – hang on, sorry, Chief Mint? Big Chief? Wait! I've got it: Director of the Imperial Mint?'

'No,' said Flippus, because he wasn't.

'Oh.' The guard took a step back, confused.

Kraaarkk! *Hurr hurr hurr!* I was perched on Flippus's shoulder, laughing my beak off.

'What's that raven doing?' snapped the leader of the Guard.

'Nothing,' said Flippus defensively.

'I'm laughin',' I said, 'because you're very funny.'

'It's against the law to laugh at the Imperial Guard,' said the soldier.

I fixed the man with one beady eye and drew myself up to my full height. 'Actually, that is not so. Roman law applies to human beings. As you can see, I'm a bird and therefore above the law, not to mention human beings, cos I can fly. *Hurr hurr hurr!* Not only that but I'm a raven, *Corvus maximus intelligentissimussimussimussimus*, the most intelligent bird there is and certainly the most intelligent creature here at this particular moment.'

And after that little speech I bowed. Am I clever or am I super-clever? No, I am mega-super-clever. Go on, give us a biscuit!

The leader of the Guard stared at me and then at Flippus Floppus. 'Who taught him to speak like that?' he demanded.

Before Flippus could speak, I clapped one wing over his mouth and answered the question myself.

'I have the honour of bein' a pupil of the best teacher in Rome, that is to say, Thesaurus.'

The guard grinned broadly. 'Thesaurus! I

might've known.
He's never short of
a word or three. OK,
Mr *Corvus minimus maximus moximus*, if you and your friend here would just let us pass, we have business with the head of the household. Krysis! Krysis!'

The soldiers pushed past us and began searching the villa. Some went upstairs, some went downstairs and one of them went to the loo.

It didn't take them long to discover Krysis and Flavia beneath the table, probably because

Krysis's feet were sticking out in full view.

Krysis tried to take control, which is a difficult thing to do when you're on your knees under a large table.

'How dare you demand anything of me!' he shouted, struggling to his feet. 'I am the Director of the Imperial Mint and I will not be spoken to like this.'

'We have orders to search your villa,' said the leader of the Guard.

'Search my villa? Whatever for? Don't be ludicrous.'

'I'm not Ludicrus. He's Ludicrus,' said the officer, pointing at one of the other guards. 'I'm Plausible, Chief Guard, and I have here a written warrant to search your villa, signed by the Emperor Tyrannus himself, with his very own name and in his very own handwriting. Money has gone missing from the Imperial Mint and we intend to find it!'

'Ohhhhh!' sighed Flavia and fainted. Her slave, Fussia, rushed over.

'My mistress!' cried Fussia and she promptly fainted too.

Flippus Floppus looked at the two prone women on the floor, waved his hands rather uselessly, said '*Mwaaaah!*' for some strange reason and then he fainted. I thought I might as well join in so I flapped about on the floor for a few moments and gave a few feeble squawks, but nobody paid any attention. (Making a joke that nobody notices is very embarrassing.)

Meanwhile, the guards carried on stomping about the house, upstairs, downstairs, downstairs, upstairs, round and round. They looked under, over, inside and outside EVERYTHING.

A shout came from a passageway. 'There's someone hiding in this room, sir!' yelled a guard.

'They've locked themselves in!' He banged on the door. 'Come on out! You're under arrest!'

All the other guards rushed to the locked door and crouched round it, ready to pounce. A timid voice spoke from the other side.

'All right, I'm coming out. Please don't hurt me.'

The door was unlocked and it slowly opened, bit by little bit. A tousled head with a very worried face peeped out.

'It's only me,' said the tall guard. 'I needed the loo.'

Before Plausible had time to tell everyone how useless they were, there was another shout, this time from one of the upstairs bedrooms.

'Sir! I've found something!'

We all raced up the stairs, apart from Flavia, Fussia and Flippus Floppus, who were still in fainting positions, and me because I can't run. I flapped.

We got to the main bedroom where Ludicrus

was holding a large bag. He opened the top and tipped it upside down. A stream of silver coins cascaded noisily on to the bed. Krysis groaned in disbelief and for a moment I thought he'd faint too.

Plausible turned to him. 'Your deputy at the Imperial Mint, Fibbus Biggus, reported this morning that ten thousand silver *denarii* had disappeared from the Mint. It was suggested that the money could've been taken by you. The Emperor therefore ordered the search and it has proved to be true. This is the stolen money. Krysis, I am arresting you for the theft of ten thousand silver *denarii* from the Emperor's Mint. Your villa and all your money will be confiscated. Your family will be thrown out on to the street and your name will be besmidged forever.'

Krysis frowned. 'Besmidged? What does that mean?'

'It means besmidged,' snapped Plausible. 'Guards, put him in chains and take him away to jail. The rest of you, you have one hour to leave this house. Forever.'

Krysis collapsed and this time *I* almost fainted! This was COMPLETELY unexpected. What was going on?

An hour later we were all sitting outside the villa on the pavement. Obviously, I wasn't sitting because birds can't sit, as you well know. I stood. There was complete silence, even from me. We were stunned. We had no bed, no food, no home, no money and no Krysis. Even worse, there were NO MORE BISCUITS! DISASTER!

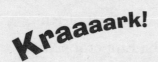

Kraaaark!

2. Ipso Facto What?

People wandered past, staring at us. Horses
went past, staring at us. Even
the donkeys stared at
us. Definitely very
annoying. It's rude
to stare – everyone knows
that, except most of Rome
it would seem. One old
man simply stood there,
looking at us.

'What's the matter, Fish-Face?' I croaked at
him and he began to splutter.

'How, how, how, how dare you! I have not got a
fish face!' he yelled.

'You could've fooled me,' I clacked. 'Your face
looks like an octopus turned inside out.'

'Hah!' he exploded. 'Hah! Hah! An octopus isn't a fish. It's a cephalopod. So there!'

'Hah! Hah!' I echoed. 'Cephalopod-Face!'

The old man slapped his head and jumped up and down. 'I can't believe I'm arguing with a wretched raven!'

'I'm not the least bit wretched, thank you very much. My feathers are glossy, my beak is clean, my eyes are bright and shiny. In other words, I present myself in prime condition and therefore I am not wretched.'

'*Bucco!*' Mr Octopus-Turned-Inside-Out-Face cackled before hurrying off with a big grin on his face.

Bucco? Hmmm. That's your actual street Latin, that is, and I'm not sure I should tell you what it means, but I shall. Do you know what he called me? A big mouth. Me! A big mouth! Can you believe it?

Whaddya mean, it's true? So I'm a big mouth now, am I, after all those nice things I said about you? Well, you can bloomin' well give me back that biscuit. In fact, you can give me any biscuits you've got and then I might consider – only consider, mind you – forgiving you.

Anyhow, where was I? Oh yes. *Ahem, ahem.* (That's me clearing my honker in order to bring you up to date on our unfortunate position.)

There we were on the street, surrounded by what little bits and bobs we'd managed to gather together before the Imperial Guard threw us out. Even I had my bit of baggage, namely a dead squirrel I'd hidden under the roof tiles for eating later.

Whaddya mean, eating squirrels is disgusting? It's what ravens do. *Corvus munchus muchia.* Squirrels, rats, worms, slugs, beetles – BISCUITS! Get over it!

Hysteria was sobbing. (Some things never change.) Perilus was on his feet and telling his mother that he would look after everyone.

'Now that Pater is in jail, I am the man of the house,' he declared, sticking his chin out as far as he could in an attempt to look brave and unconquerable.

Flavia honoured him with a weak smile. 'Yes, dear,' she murmured. 'I'm sure you'll do a grand job. Do you think you could start by looking after your sister?'

Perilus glanced at Hysteria. She'd been sobbing for such a long time I was amazed she hadn't actually drowned.

'Hysteria!' Perilus said, rather sharply I thought. 'Put a cork in it!'

Hysteria looked up at her younger brother,

stopped sobbing, shouted, 'Put a cork in it yourself!' back at him and went back to weeping.

'I can't stop thinking about poor Scorcha, still languishing in jail,' she moaned. 'He's in a damp, dark, dim dump of a dungeon, with no food.'

Suddenly she brightened and dried her eyes. 'I could make him a snack and take it to him and he'll be SO grateful he'll fall in love with me forever and ever and we'll get married.'

Flavia reached out and put a consoling hand on Hysteria's arm. 'Hysteria, darling, we don't have any food for ourselves, let alone Scorcha. Besides, people don't fall in love with you just because you've made them a sandwich. Anyhow, we don't have a kitchen. In fact, we don't have a house. We're living on the street from now on. But never mind, darling. I expect they make lovely cakes in prison. I'm sure there'll be a little cafe in there with cupcakes and icing and maybe even cherries on top.'

'*WAAAAAAAAAAAAA!*' Oh dear. Hysteria

wasn't the least bit convinced. Neither was I, or anyone else for that matter who wasn't living in Flavia's dreamworld. Hysteria threw herself back into sobbing. Honestly, that girl is a walking waterfall. (OK, more of a sitting-down waterfall just at the moment.)

'We have to get Pater out of jail,' insisted Perilus.

'Yes, dear,' said Flavia sweetly. 'How shall we do that?'

'I'll think of something,' Perilus declared. He stuck his chin out again and half closed his eyes

to show how hard he was thinking.

I sighed. I was getting jealous of the boy. He looked so manly with his chin jutting out, and no matter how clever I am – and I don't have to remind you that I am very, VERY clever – I'm still a bird, a raven, and, *ipso facto*, I don't have a chin to stick out.

Yes, it's the old Latin popping up again. I like this one. *Ipso facto* kind of means 'because of what I've just said it follows that . . .' See what I mean? Because I'm a bird I don't have a chin. Try it for yourself. The next time your teacher asks you where your homework is, all you have to do is say: 'I did the work, but Dad was hungry and he tore it from my book and ate it and then he got squashed by an elephant looking for somewhere to sit down and unfortunately he thought my dad was a chair. *Ipso facto*, I can't show it to you.'

Your teacher will be SO impressed, she or he (or it! *Hurr hurr hurr!*) will give you six smiley faces and a choccy bar, I bet. Talking of which, have you got any biscuits? Getting a bit starvatious here.

Whaddya mean, 'starvatious' isn't a word? I KNOW THAT! Don't forget I'm a pupil of the great, the one and only Thesaurus, who knows more words than the biggest dictionary in the world.

Anyhow, things were looking grim for my poor family, but then they got grimmer. Who should come sneaking across the road but Crabbus, our neighbour from the other side of the street.

In case you haven't met Crabbus before, I'd better explain. He's married to Septicaemia and most people call them The Ghastlies because that's exactly what they are. They're mean, nasty and basically about as unpleasant as two sharks with toothache. They also think that they're better than anyone else on their side of the street because they have one slave. ONE! Putuponn is the poor girl's name.

Anyhow, Crabbus came slinking across to us, a slimy grin on his bleary face.

'Oh look!' he sneered. 'How are the mighty fallen! Daddy been putting his sticky fingers in the Emperor's pot of gold, eh?'

'Pater is innocent!' yelled Perilus furiously.

'Oooh! Innocent, is he? Where have I heard that one before? He's just like all the rest of you rich big nobs. Well, look at you now: down and out with nowhere to live. Ha ha ha! Serves you right. I always knew you lot were trash, despite all your slaves and your fine clothes and fancy food.'

Crabbus went back to his house, still grinning. Huh. I'd like to peck out his eyes. Oh no, I'm talking about food again and my stomach's beginning to rumble.

Whaddya mean, surely ravens don't eat eyeballs? Of course we do. That's the tastiest bit! No, it's not disgusting; it's what ravens do, OK? Besides, what do you eat? Stuffed dormice! Big Roman favourite. You think that's nice – all those cute little furry things, stuffed and cooked, and you gobbling away at them as if they're crisps?

Anyhow, no sooner had that slimeball Crabbus gone back inside than Trendia came trotting across to us, looking concerned. Now Trendia is someone I do have time for. She's lovely and is Scorcha's landlady. He rents a room from her. In fact, they live in the same building as Crabbus and Septicaemia. She's also a seamstress and a widow. (Her husband was a soldier in the army, but he had a nasty accident with an enemy's sword. Basically, he got stuck on the wrong end of it and died as a result. You get the point? GET THE POINT! I crack myself up sometimes, although I don't suppose He thought it was funny at the time.)

'I heard what happened,' she said. 'I can't believe it. Is it true? Krysis is in jail?'

Flavia silently nodded.

'He's innocent.' Perilus clenched his fists.

'I'm sure of that,' said Trendia. 'But you can't stay out here on the street.'

'There's nowhere else for us to go.' Flavia stared helplessly at her hands. 'I don't know what to do.'

'I do.' Trendia began to pick up some of our baggage. 'Come with me,' she said. 'You're going to stay in my house, at least until we can find you rooms of your own. Don't worry. We'll sort you out.'

Ah! Lovely, kind Trendia, our lifesaver! I looked at her with shiny, adoring eyes.

'Trendia, beautiful lady! I don't suppose you've got any biscuits on you?'

Kraaaark!

3. How to Throw a Wobbly, Big Time!

The good thing about moving house was that we
had very little to move, just our clothes, or, in my
case, my feathers. Ever seen a raven in a toga?
Nope. Nor have I – not that it wouldn't suit me. I
think I'd look rather resplendent. I could become
Emperor. I'd make a better job of it than most
Emperors we've had. *Toc-toc-toc.* (That's the noise
us ravens make when we're feeling satisfied with
ourselves.)

The bad thing about moving was that, despite
Trendia's kind offer of shelter, we were now all
crammed into one tiny room. Moving around was
impossible. I was all right, perched on top of a
cupboard, but down below people were crawling
between legs or clambering over one another.
The place was heaving. It was like looking down

at a bowl of overly large maggots. Aargh! No! I'm thinking about food again! (Maggots are VERY tasty, if you happen to be a raven.)

There was nothing I could do to help and, besides, I'd been doing a lot of thinking. We were in an awkward position, in more ways than one. Krysis was in prison and he'd had his villa taken

away from him AND all his money, so what were the rest of us going to live on?

We knew Krysis hadn't taken any money from the Imperial Mint. It simply wasn't the sort of thing he'd do. Krysis has his faults, but he's not a thief. So, if Krysis hadn't taken the money, who had? And how did it end up in our villa?

I also happened to know that the Emperor likes Krysis. They're friends. After all, Tyrannus had once suggested that his brainless daughter Clumpia might marry Perilus! So what exactly was going on?

There were a lot of questions that needed answering so I decided I'd pay the Emperor a flying visit. (*Hurr hurr hurr!* Raven joke! A *flying* visit! Got it? Of course you have.)

Getting into the palace was easy and I found Tyrannus lolling on a divan, being fed grapes by a young slave. That made me sigh and roll my eyes. I mean, what a cliché!

I saluted him with one wing. '*Salve*, Tyrannus!'

'Ah, Croakbag. *Salve.* Fancy a grape?' Tyrannus clicked his fingers and the slave put a bunch of fine black grapes right in front of me. Very nice too. The Emperor of Rome raised one eyebrow rather sardonically, so I adopted the same attitude. I cocked my head on one side and fixed him with my beadiest, one-eyed stare.

'I see you're up to your usual tricks, Tyrannus,' I croaked.

'Really? What can you possibly mean, you black-hearted rogue?'

'Throwin' Krysis and his family on to the streets,' I said bluntly.

Tyrannus shrugged. 'What else could I do? Fibbus Biggus reported that money had been stolen from the Mint. When questioned, he was asked who might have taken it and suggested that Krysis was in the best position to commit the crime.'

I shook my head. 'You know as well as I do that Krysis would never do such a thing.'

'Do I? Do I know that? Is there proof? Do you know who the thief is?'

'Not yet.'

'Then the family will have to stay on the street until the thief is found,' the Emperor declared.

'Krysis is in jail,' I pointed out.

'Lucky man,' drawled Tyrannus. 'I could have had him thrown to the Colosseum lions.'

'Exactly.' I smiled. Now I had Tyrannus just where I wanted him. 'You could've done just that. But you didn't, did you? You didn't because you know that he's not guilty.'

I gave my wings a little shake to show Tyrannus

I was right. He looked at me for a long time before speaking again.

'That might be so,' he agreed. 'All right, I admit it: I don't think Krysis is guilty. Nevertheless, the money was found in his bedroom. What could I do but put him in jail? It would've looked very odd if I hadn't. I couldn't let him carry on as Director of the Imperial Mint. I've appointed Fibbus Biggus. He'll take over.'

'Fibbus Big—!' I couldn't even bring myself to finish his name. I was choking. 'That buffoon?' This was a blow – a big blow – but Tyrannus was right. Someone had to run the Mint. I sighed and pressed on. 'But you must want the real thief found, and the best person to do that is Krysis himself. If the real thief knew Krysis was out there searchin' for him, then he might well do somethin' stupid and draw attention to himself without realizin'.' The trap would be sprung and the real thief caught. '*Toc-toc-toc.*' I added, with satsifaction. I'm so clever.

34

The Emperor nodded. 'I knew you were smart, Croakbag,' he remarked. 'But you're sly as well. You could be right. Krysis does need to be out there on the trail of the real thief. It would help Flavia and the children too. I shall consider it.'

'Thank you,' I said, because good manners always, always help things along, especially when you're talking to Emperors. I picked up the grapes that were left, crammed them into my beak and departed.

'*Vale*, Croakbag!' the Emperor shouted after me as I left.

'*Va–*' I squawked in reply and of course all the grapes fell out of my beak.

Tyrannus laughed. 'Not so clever after all, *Corvus maximus intelligentissimus*!'

I shan't tell you what I shouted back at him.

By the time I got back to Trendia's place, big changes were going on. Maddasbananus had come up with an idea. Maddasbananus lives in the apartment next to Trendia. He's an inventor and he's barking mad if you ask me – always inventing stuff that doesn't work. Nevertheless, he's a good man and he rather likes Trendia, but is too shy to say anything.

Anyhow, Maddasbananus had seen Flavia and family cramming themselves into Trendia's place and wondered what was going on. When he found out, he made a startlingly good suggestion.

'Why don't you move in upstairs? There are at least three or four empty rooms up there.'

Trendia looked at the inventor, her eyes like little stars in a heavenly sky. (I really should've been a poet.)

'That is SUCH a good idea, Maddasbananus!'

The inventor turned scarlet and sighed. Honestly, was he lovesick or not? (Yes, he was.)

So everyone went up the wooden steps at one end of the big house to explore the apartments. Maddasbananus was right: the rooms were empty. They were also dark and dusty. The floorboards creaked. The doors squeaked and so did Hysteria.

'It's awful, Mater. These rooms are so – dirty. Urgh!'

Trendia looked at Flavia. 'What do you think?' she asked, as Perilus and Hysteria went on ahead, exploring the other rooms.

I knew what Flavia was thinking, even if nobody else did. She was remembering that a few hours earlier she'd been living in a swanky villa and now she was being offered four dirty little rooms barely big enough for a rat. (And there probably were rats, judging by the droppings I could not only see but smell.)

But Flavia didn't let on. She jutted out her chin.

It was obviously a family habit, all this chin-jutting. 'With a bit of a clean, these rooms *could* be fine.'

'But what about the rent, Mater?' Perilus wanted to know.

'I'm sure we'll find a way,' Flavia murmured. She's such an optimist.

'We can help a bit,' Trendia said, glancing across at Maddasbananus, and he nodded.

Do you see? Do you see how kind people can be when they know someone's in trouble? You won't find Emperors offering that sort of help, or rich men. When someone needs help, where does it come from? The poor. The poor would share their last meal with you if they thought you were hungry. You won't find your senators and consuls offering so much as a grape. No, no, they're far above things like that. Makes me proud to know people like Maddasbananus and Trendia. Salt of the earth, that's what they are. Brings tears to my beady little eyes, thinking about their kindness. *Sniff, sniff.*

I was in the middle of drowning in my own sentimental pool when Hysteria came rushing back and began tugging at her mother.

'We cannot possibly live up here!' she cried. 'Have you seen the room next door? It's worse than a pigsty – worse than a hundred pigsties. Just come and look at it, Mater!'

Hysteria pulled Flavia through to the next room and we all followed. Perilus was standing in the middle, surrounded by piles of rat droppings and twigs from old nests. Broken plaster from the walls now lay on the floor. Bits of straw mattress were scattered all over the place. Cockroaches were beetling about the floor and we were just in time to see a pair of rats scuttle away through a small hole in the wall. The floorboards that could actually be seen were completely rotten with woodworm.

Hysteria went and stood next to Perilus. Her eyes filled with tears as she worked herself up into a good old-fashioned wobbly fit. 'Oh, Mater! Isn't

it ghastly? How can we possibly live in a dump like this? It's utterly, UTTERLY appalling!' And she stamped her little feet. Hysteria's feet may well be little, but it was a BIG MISTAKE because the rotten floor beneath those little feet gave way. There was an almighty crash as several floorboards broke. A huge cloud of dust and splinters of wood billowed up. In a flash, Perilus and

Hysteria both disappeared from view as they fell through the hole into the room beneath.

There was a loud scream (from Hysteria) and an even louder yell (from Perilus), closely followed by an explosion of angry voices.

We rushed to the edge of the hole and peered down, coughing furiously from the cloud of dust that was swirling around us.

Down below, an extraordinary sight met our eyes. Immediately below us we saw Perilus and Hysteria clutching each other. They were sitting plonk in the middle of a broken table, with squashed food spread all around them. In fact, Hysteria appeared to be sitting in a bowl of soup. (It turned out it *was* a bowl of soup.) At one end of the table, Septicaemia had fallen backwards on her chair and was now struggling to free herself from her *stola*, her chair and the pile of washing she had fallen into. At the other end of the table, Crabbus was lying on the floor, face down, with his head buried in a cooked chicken. All four of them were yelling.

It seemed that The Ghastlies had just sat down to some lunch when Hysteria and Perilus fell through the rotten floorboards in the room above and landed, *SPLAP!*, right in the middle of the dinner table, breaking it and sending The Ghastlies crashing to the ground. Laugh? I almost died! *Hurr hurr hurr!* Give 'em a biscuit! It might cheer 'em up. **Kraaaarrkk!**

4. Another Big Surprise –
But a Good One. Hooray!

'I'm fed up to the back teeth with you lot!' roared
Crabbus. 'Look what you've done! I'm going
to tell the magistrate about this. I shall tell the
Senate – the Emperor himself will get to hear of
it. You'll all be thrown to the lions and it'll serve
you right. You can't go around smashing up other
people's property!'

'Yeah!' screamed Septicaemia. 'You're vandals,
you are! All of you!'

'*Ahem, ahem.*' (That's me clearing my throat.) '*Ahem*. Actually, Septicaemia, we are definitely not vandals. The Vandals, as you should know, are a tribe of people from Germania. They don't always behave well and that's where the word "vandal" comes from. That's a fact. *Ergo*, we are not vandals. We're Romans, just like you and Crabbus. Even I, a raven, am a Roman raven, *Corvus Romanus certus*, which translates as "Certainly a raven from Rome". So there. *Toc-toc-toc.*' And I clacked with considerable satisfaction and rustling of glossy black feathers.

Ergo – that's your actual Latin and it means 'therefore'. Nice one, eh? Try that one on your Dad and amaze him with your intelligence.

Anyhow, my little speech was greeted with stunned silence, but it didn't last long because Crabbus was on his high horse again.

Whaddya mean, you didn't know Crabbus had a tall horse and why hadn't I mentioned it before? It wasn't a real horse – it's an expression!

44

Of course he doesn't have a horse and even if he did he wouldn't keep it indoors, would he?

'What are you waffling on about, you black bag of burps?' Crabbus shouted.

'Just explainin' things,' I pointed out calmly.

'One day,' hissed Septicaemia, her eyes like knives, 'I am going to cook that bird and eat it!'

I carefully took a few steps away from the snake.

'Crabbus, this was quite simply an accident. The floorboards were rotten and gave way. How was anyone to know that would happen? We'll help you clear up.'

Now you may be wondering why I made this kind offer. Did I mention a cooked chicken earlier? Said chicken was still lying on the floor. I could see it, I could smell it and, unlike the rat droppings upstairs, it smelled good. Oh, so, so good!

'Accident?' repeated Crabbus. He waved both arms at the broken table, the squashed food and general mess that covered the floor and went halfway up the walls. Not to mention the plague of cockroaches Hysteria and Perilus had brought down with them. 'I don't care if it was an accident. What were those kids doing upstairs anyway? Trespassing, that's what they were doing. Entering property they had no right to go into.'

Flavia glided forward. 'We are going to rent the rooms upstairs, Crabbus. That's why we were up there. When you rent rooms, you always take a look at them first.'

Septicaemia started hissing again and I moved even further away from her. 'You! Rent those rooms! Do you think you can just swan over here and rent rooms in this house? YOU HAVEN'T GOT ANY MONEY NOW, MRS FLAVIA!' she shouted. 'You and your family are nothing. You're nobodies without a single *denarius* to your name. YOU'RE BEGGARS! Get back out there on the street. You've nothing to pay the rent with and nobody to pay it for you!'

Flavia was almost reduced to tears by this nasty outburst. Even if what Septicaemia had said was true, she needn't have said it so viciously, so triumphantly. She was like a snake swallowing its prey.

'Actually, dear Septicaemia,' said a deep voice from behind us, 'we *shall* be renting those rooms and *I* will be paying the rent.'

Everyone, including me, whizzed round to stare in amazement at the newcomer. Guess who it was? You can't? OK, I shall tell you. It was Krysis. What a surprise! There he was, standing in the doorway and holding up a small bag which he shook so that the money inside jingled.

Crabbus spat on the floor at Krysis's feet and a sneer slid on to his pasty face. 'Oh! Been stealing again, have you?'

Krysis stepped right up to him. 'You really are a piece of dirt, Crabbus. This is money I lent to a friend two years ago and he has now paid me back. I've been released from prison by the Emperor with no charge against me. I would've been here sooner, but I thought I'd better try and find some money first of all. We are going to rent the rooms upstairs, Crabbus, and we will get the rotten floor mended. Now then, would you like to spit at my feet again or would you prefer to apologize, both of you, for speaking to Flavia and me so unpleasantly?'

Great Jupiter above! I never would've thought Krysis would say something like that. I have to say I was impressed. I always knew Krysis was a good man, but he fights with words, not fists, and here he was, facing up to a man taller, wider and a mean bully.

'Darling!' cried Flavia, rushing across to him and kissing his face umpteen times. I'm surprised he had any face left after she'd washed it so much.

'*Pater!*' cried Hysteria, rushing across to him and hugging him.

'Hi, Pater,' murmured Perilus, not rushing anywhere near him and keeping his hands in the pockets of his food-stained tunic.

Whaddya mean, you bet tunics didn't have pockets? How would you know? Who's the expert, eh? Me, that's who. *Corvus maximus experticus.* If I say Perilus's tunic had pockets, then that's that. Get over it!

So Perilus was playing it cool, but Hysteria was still clinging to her father. 'Did you see Scorcha in jail? Is he all right? Does he have food? Did he say he missed – erm, anyone?' she added hopefully.

Krysis sighed. 'Yes, I saw Scorcha and he said he misses the chariot racing. He's got a bit scruffy and dirty and he smells.'

'Oh! Poor Scorcha!' gasped Hysteria, on the edge of tears. 'He must be awfully thin and scrawny now, wasting away. He needs food and a good wash. Poor, poor Scorcha!' And she began to sob quietly.

I know, it's tiresome, isn't it, all this weeping and wailing? I wouldn't mind if it was just every so often, but with Hysteria it's more like every than often, if you get my meaning.

'I'm definitely going to take him some food,' Hysteria suddenly announced during a brief interval in this tearful downpour.

50

'Good idea,' I said. 'Best get on with it and take your time.'

So Hysteria hurried off to prepare a five-course dinner for the handsome young (and wasting away, not to mention smelly) charioteer.

'I'll help you, Hysteria!' Trendia called after her. 'You can have some food from my kitchen!' The pair went hurrying off, nattering away like best buddies.

Flavia gazed lovingly at her husband. 'Why did the Emperor decide to let you go?' she asked.

I rubbed my chest with one wing and strutted up and down proudly. After all, that had been my amazing work. 'Yes,' I cawed. 'Do tell us why the Emperor released you.'

'Tyrannus said he didn't want to see an old friend rot in jail. I think he knows I'm not guilty, but he can't do much else until I find out who the real thief is. Meanwhile, the villa and our money remain confiscated.' Krysis stared hard at the ground and nodded. 'I have to find that thief.'

'*Ahem, ahem,*' I coughed quietly. 'And what else did the Emperor say?' I prompted, steadying myself to receive an avalanche of high praise for my incredible achievement in getting Krysis out of jail.

'There wasn't anything else.' Krysis looked puzzled.

'What?!' I almost fainted. In fact, I don't think I've ever been so close to fainting in my entire life. I really did have to steady myself now. I could feel my knees trembling and I hoped nobody would notice. 'Didn't the Emperor mention ME – AT ALL?'

'Oh! Yes, of course, I almost forgot,' said Krysis and his face lit up at the memory. 'He also said, "Tell that rascal raven of yours he's a greedy, big-headed blabber-beak."'

'Oh, he did, did he?' I said, pulling myself up to my full, imposing height of fifty-five centimetres. 'He said that? Well, if you ever see that tinpot, tiddly-eyed Tyrannus again, you can tell him he's a –'

But I never got to say what I was going to say about Tyrannus because Hysteria interrupted me. She was standing at the door, clutching a small packet.

'I'm going to take Scorcha this food,' she declared with delight. 'I can't bear to think of him suffering.'

'Lovely, darling,' Flavia beamed. 'I'm sure he'll be very pleased.'

'Yes, bye-bye!' I called after Hysteria as she left. Phew. Thank Jupiter! No more sobbing for a little while at least.

'Croakbag,' said Flavia, 'would you go with her, please, just to keep an eye on her?'

Huh. Just when I was ready for some peace and quiet. 'Can't Fussia go? She is her slave, after all, and I'm not. I'm a raven.'

'I need Fussia to clean the floors,' Flavia said.

'Send Flippus Floppus then.'

'He's washing the walls.'

'What about Perilus?' I asked.

'He's needed here too. Now be a dear and go and keep an eye on Hysteria. When you come back, you may have a biscuit.'

'Two biscuits,' I demanded imperiously.

'One,' said Flavia sweetly. 'Nobody wants a fat raven, do they? You'd never take off.'

Oh, Flavia! She always seems so concerned for my well-being. What could I do? Nothing. I simply sighed and went flapping off after Hysteria. As things turned out, it was a very good thing I did too. What would that family do without me? Sink, sink without trace, that's what. They would sink like an overloaded and rudderless ship, snatched away by the Currents of Calamity and sucked down into the Darkest Depths of Despair by the Whirlpool of Destiny.

You see? I really should've been a poet. Or a politician. Go on, give us a biscuit! Flavia won't.

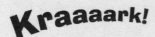

5. Hysteria's Clever Plan – and Other Problems

'Why are you following me?' Hysteria demanded, as she hurried towards the Imperial Prison.

'I'm not followin' you. It just so happens that we're both goin' in the same direction.'

'Same difference,' Hysteria shot back.

'As I've told you many times, Hysteria, there is no such thing as the same difference between two things. Two things are either the same or they're different. They cannot have the same difference. You need at least three things in order to have the same difference between them and then, in any case, they would be the same differences, with an "s" on the end, thus makin' it plural.'

Hysteria stopped and fixed me with an angry glare. 'It's no wonder people throw stones at you.

Tyrannus was right. You're a big-headed blabber-beak.'

'Very well, I'll shut up. You go ahead.'

Huh. The ungrateful creature. All I did was explain things to her. You'd think she'd be pleased. I almost decided to go back to the new apartments, but then I remembered how dingy and uncomfortable they were so I carried on following Little Miss Waterfall.

When she got to the jail, she asked to see Scorcha.

'Why?' asked the big, bulgy guard.

'I've brought some food for him,' Hysteria explained.

'Have you got anything hidden in it?'

'Like what?' she asked.

'Swords, knives, sharp objects that might be used to gouge out my eyes, files for filing through prison bars, pliers, hammers, catapults, battering rams, suitcases for hiding in, exploding things or frogs.'

'Frogs?' repeated Hysteria.

'Can't stand 'em. They're really scary and make me suck my thumb.'

'I haven't got anything like that,' Hysteria told him indignantly.

'OK, you may pass.' And he let her in.

I swooped down and landed beside the guard. 'You're scared of frogs? You should try eatin' them. Very nice.'

The guard jumped about a mile in the air. 'Jupiter save me! It's a talking raven!'

I sighed. 'Of course I can talk. *Corvus maximus intelligentissimus.* Get over it!' And I flapped off to see what Hysteria was up to.

She had found Scorcha. Now you haven't forgotten that Hysteria has a BIG CRUSH on Scorcha, have you? Of course not. You are, after all, almost as intelligent as I am.

Whaddya mean, you're much *more* intelligent because you're human? Huh! You've got to be joking. You might have a bigger brain than me, but what do you use it for? Boasting. Arguing. Fighting. Wars. Whereas I use mine for finding interesting places to hide dead squirrels and rats and other deceased creatures that I might want to nibble on when hunger strikes. Now that's what I call a sensible use of the noddle. But let us continue.

It's hardly surprising Hysteria had fallen for Scorcha. After all, the lad is young, handsome, strong, muscular and a mighty fine charioteer.

'You're safe!' she cried.

'Sort of,' Scorcha said. 'Well, I'm not exactly going anywhere, am I? How are things?'

'We've been thrown out of the villa.'

Scorcha nodded. 'I know. Krysis told me. Sorry.'

'We're living in the same house as Trendia,' Hysteria told him.

'That's, um, nice?'

'The rooms are a bit crummy, but it's better than being on the street, and I'm closer to you.' Hysteria smiled up at him and fluttered her long eyelashes. That old trick. 'I've brought you some food. It's leftovers from yesterday, but it should be all right.'

'Oh. Thanks. Looks all right. Mmmm. Tastes all right.'

'I made it myself,' murmured Hysteria happily. 'For you.'

'Hmmm,' Scorcha grunted as he chewed. Eventually, he swallowed and began muttering. 'I've got to get out of here, Hysteria. There are chariot races tomorrow and the Green Team, my team, they want me there to race for them. Their captain, Jellus, is useless and they want me to take his place. It's my big chance to show the Greens what I can do, instead of which I'm stuck here in this dingy dungeon.'

Hysteria suddenly grabbed Scorcha's arm. 'I can get you out!' she whispered. '*I can get you out!*'

'You just said that,' Scorcha answered.

'I know. It's because I'm excited. You MUST race tomorrow!'

'But Hysteria, how are you going to get me out?'

Aha! Just what I was wondering.

Hysteria clapped her little hands and explained. 'It's simple. We swop clothes. You pretend to be me and walk out. Then I follow you a little later.'

Scorcha thought for a short while and then frowned. 'Suppose it fails?'

Hysteria shook her head. 'Then things will just

stay the same. But it won't fail. You'll be free!'

Hmmm. There was something that bothered me about Hysteria's plan, but I couldn't quite put my wing on exactly what it was. I kept running it through my head while the two of them began exchanging clothes.

'You're not looking, are you?' asked Hysteria.

'I've got your *stola* stuck over my head and I can't see a thing,' mumbled Scorcha.

Hysteria pulled it down for him and in a few minutes they were ready. Scorcha had Hysteria's clothes on and she was

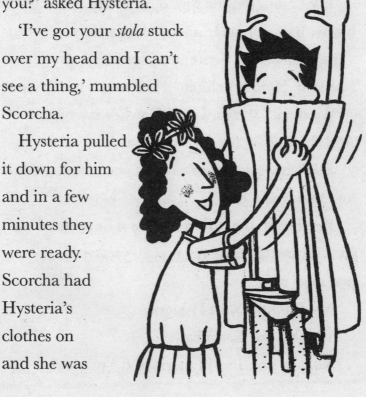

wearing his tunic. Very fetching too. *Toc-toc-toc.*

Hysteria pushed Scorcha towards the door. 'Go on. Just pretend to be me and walk out.'

And that is exactly what Scorcha did. He approached the frog-fearing guard at the door.

'*Vale,*' he said in what he hoped was a squeaky, girly voice.

'*Vale,*' muttered the guard, who was bored to bits with the whole business of guarding.

We watched as Scorcha disappeared to freedom. Hysteria clutched her hands in triumph.

'We did it!' she told me. 'Now it's my turn.' And she walked towards the guard.

'*Vale,*' she murmured in what she hoped was a low, manly voice.

'*Va—*' began the guard and then he pointed his spear at her. 'Hang on, you can't leave. You're a prisoner.'

'No, I'm not,' said Hysteria.

'Yes, you are, Scorcha.'

'No, I'm not. I'm Hysteria and I'm a girl.'

'You're wearing a boy's tunic,' the guard pointed out.

'And you're wearing a skirt,' Hysteria said. 'But that doesn't make you a girl.'

'All soldiers wear skirts. It's our uniform.'

'It's a girly uniform,' Hysteria argued.

'Really? Do you think so? I've always thought I looked quite manly.'

'You're not manly. You're scared of frogs,' said Hysteria.

'Yeah, well, that might be so, but you're getting on my nerves and I'm not letting you out because you are Scorcha and he's a prisoner. Now get back inside.'

'But I'm a girl!' Hysteria insisted and her eyes started to well up.

Uh-oh. Here we go, I thought. *Blub blub blub.* Hysteria even tried to wipe her tears on the soldier's 'skirt', as she called it.

'Oy! You can stop that!' he growled. 'That's misuse of government property. Go on, back inside, you!' He pushed Hysteria into the jail and slammed the door shut.

So there we have it: Scorcha had escaped, but Hysteria was now in jail in his place. I guess you could call that fifty per cent successful. It's a fine pickle, isn't it? Whatever next? Give 'em all a biscuit. **Kraaarrkk!**

6. A Piece-a This and a Piece-a That

Bit of a problem, but, I thought to myself, don't get your feathers in a flap, Croakbag. You can sort this out. Make a list.

Oh yes, now my brain was getting into gear! Us ravens are super-smart and I, *Corvus brainus giganticus*, am super-mega-SUPER-smart. All I had to do was itemize all the problems.

1. Scorcha was now free, but would need somewhere to hide in case he was spotted by The Ghastlies, who'd got him stuffed in jail in the first place. So, find Scorcha a hiding place and get him back to racing chariots.
2. Hysteria was now in jail instead of Scorcha. So, get Hysteria out of prison.

3. Krysis was now out of prison, but had to find out who the real thief at the Imperial Mint was. So, prove Krysis was innocent.

4. Funnily enough, problem four was lumbering down the road right at that moment.

Big wagons loaded with furniture were arriving at our old home, the villa across the road. It had barely been empty a few hours and already someone was moving in, but who? Who was rich

enough and powerful enough to take over such a luxurious home? (Six bedrooms, dining area, *vomitorium* (look it up, it's disgusting!), kitchen, four additional rooms, atrium with pool, underfloor heating, bathroom with both hot and cold plunge pools plus, outside, extensive gardens laid to lawn, garage for two carriages and stabling for several horses. Interested parties should contact the estate agents, Fabricatus, Sneakia and Grubb.)

We stood on the balcony and watched the endless parade. (That's to say, I perched – everyone else stood.) One wagon after another rolled up to the gates. Slaves unloaded chests and cupboards and beds and carried them in. Finally,

a very smart carriage appeared at the end of the road and trundled towards us. It stopped outside the villa and guess who got out?

FIBBUS BIGGUS!

Fibbus Biggus, the ex-Deputy Director of the Imperial Mint. I say ex-Deputy Director because as you know Tyrannus had appointed him to Krysis's position and Fibbus was now the Director. He was top dog. *Woof woof*, probably a poodle. *Hurr hurr hurr!* Didn't he think he was the smart and swanky one? Oh yes. He looked across at us, lifted his big Roman nose into the air as if he couldn't even bear to sniff us and walked into the villa, all *hoitus-toitus*.

Fibbus Biggus was now living in OUR VILLA! Definitely problem number four. So GET HIM OUT! Shall we give Fibbus a biscuit? DEFINITELY NOT!

KRAAARRKKK!

Hmmm, that's quite a lot for one raven to sort out, even if I am clever. Now then, you know me: I'm not one to boast. I'm a modest chap really. In fact, I'm mega-modest, but I can't deny that I am clever and quite possibly the most amazing raven ever known to the civilized world, not to mention the uncivilized world. *Corvus superbia brainus*, no less. *Toc-toc-toc.*

By way of demonstrating to you just how clever I am, I'd like to say that it was as I was watching snotty-nosed Fibbus Biggus march into OUR villa that something suddenly popped into my feathery head. WHO would benefit from Krysis being sent to prison? Ask yourself that. Are you there yet? If not, here's a clue: two letters – a great big capital 'F' and an equally great big capital 'B'. So that was something to think on.

Meantime, Krysis was moving into *his* new home. All I can say is that the villa that used to be ours was a five-star palace compared to the dump we were in now, which didn't have any stars at all, being more of a black hole. *Hurr hurr hurr!*

Nevertheless, it was the same 'dump' that Maddasbananus, Trendia and Scorcha had to live in. We were about to see how the other half lived and it wasn't a pretty sight. The walls were damp. Paint was peeling. The floors were filthy. And we won't even mention the rotten floorboards, cockroaches and rats that you already know about.

Whaddya mean, I've just mentioned them? I know that! It's a figure of speech. Get over it!

Flippus Floppus had thrown what little

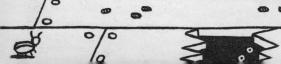

bedding he and Fussia had managed to take from the villa down into the corner of one room. I don't think I have introduced you properly to Flippus Floppus and Fussia yet, have I? They're slaves. Now before you go off screaming about the injustice of slavery let me remind you that Rome was so full of slaves that even some of the slaves had slaves. Besides, if you were lucky, like Fussia and Flippus Floppus, you might have a good, kind master and mistress, such as Krysis and Flavia.

When we were in the villa, we had five slaves altogether. Flippus and Fussia looked after Krysis and the family. A third slave did the cooking. The fourth slave looked after Flippus Floppus and Fussia. The fifth slave looked after the third and fourth slaves and herself.

There was actually a sixth slave, but he lived outside with the horses, so we don't count him.

He looked after the horses and himself. When we got thrown out of the villa, we had to leave the slaves behind, but Flippus and Fussia insisted that they wanted to stay with us. They're almost part of the family, but, as Krysis will remind you, they are still slaves.

Anyway, our new home was FILTHY, spelled with a capital 'D' for disgusting.

'We'll clean it,' said Fussia, rather bravely I thought. She threw a broom at Flippus Floppus and told him to start sweeping. Just for a moment, I couldn't tell who was what or what was who because Flippus is so thin he looks remarkably like an upside-down broom himself.

I had that list of mine to work on and I decided to start with Scorcha. Luckily, The Ghastlies, namely Crabbus and Septicaemia, had gone off to the forum market. I found Scorcha sitting in a chair and relaxing while Flavia bustled about, making some food for him.

This was usually Fussia's job, so I was

wondering why Flavia had her hands in the mixing bowl and why Scorcha was in her kitchen, still wearing Hysteria's clothes. Could it possibly be that Flavia's heart fluttered a little faster when she saw the daring charioteer? More than likely if you ask me. Handsome young charioteers are always popular with the ladies.

Anyhow, Flavia was gliding about the tiny kitchen, which was full of delicious smells. She beamed at Scorcha. 'You sit there and relax after your horrible time in prison,' she said. 'I can't imagine what it must be like for poor Hysteria. I do hope we can get her out of there soon. But you need feeding up, Scorcha, before your big race tomorrow and I'm making you a special dish I've invented and I want you to test it for me.'

'Smells good,' said Scorcha. 'What is it?'

'I'm not sure what to call it,' Flavia answered. 'I've made some very thin, flat bread and I've put a piece of this on it, and a piece of that, and a piece of something else. It's lots of pieces really.'

'Maybe you should call it a piece-a this and a piece-a that?' suggested Scorcha.

Flavia laughed. 'Piece-a for short,' she said.

'Piece-a!' repeated Scorcha, his mouth full of the first bite. He closed his eyes. 'And I declare this piece-a absolutely yummy-scrummy!'

Flavia clapped her hands in delight. 'I'm so pleased you like it. You see, it's my Big Idea. We have to earn some money now, and Krysis told me I should come up with something, so I thought I could cook things and sell them. Lots of people do that, but they all sell the same kind of things – stuffed dormice, Roman nibbles, you know? So I thought I'd try and create something different and here it is, the piece-a!'

Whaddya mean, it sounds like 'pizza'? Of course it does. It's meant to. Well done, you've worked it out. Someone had to invent the pizza, didn't they?

'*Pizza!*' declared Scorcha with extra expression, rising to his feet. 'You have given the world the

pizza! It tastes *so* good. You should sell
them at the Colosseum on race days!'

'Perfect,' nodded Flavia. 'I'll make lots
more and open a stall.'

Well, those two obviously didn't need my
help, did they? Oh, hang on: we had to keep
Scorcha out of sight of The Ghastlies.

I swooped down, pinched a bit of pizza
and my oh my!
Was that tasty?
Hmmm-mmmmm! It
most certainly was. After
all, one can get tired
of dead squirrel. But
there were important
matters to discuss.

'We have to keep
you hidden, Scorcha.
Krysis and his family
need this space and,
besides, The Ghastlies

will soon find out you're here otherwise. We need to keep you out of sight and find a way to get you to the Colosseum on race days without anyone spottin' you. Maybe Maddasbananus has somewhere.'

'That crazy inventor?' Scorcha gave a loud guffaw.

'*Toc-toc-toc.* He's not crazy, Scorcha. It's his inventions that are mad. Have you seen his Time Machine? It's a wardrobe with an hour-glass on the top. He reckons all the sand in the bottom of the timer is The Past so, when you turn it over, The Past runs back into The Present and therefore you go back in Time.'

Scorcha laughed again. 'Like I said, Maddasbananus is crazy.'

I shook my head and was about to say more when we were interrupted by the arrival of Krysis and Perilus. Perilus was amazed to see his great friend Scorcha sitting there as large as life.

'You're free!' he cried. 'What happened?'

I explained. 'He escaped by changin' clothes with Hysteria. Unfortunately, the fish-for-brains guard now thinks that Hysteria is Scorcha, so it's your sister who's in prison.'

Perilus smiled. 'Fantastic! No more wailing round the house!'

'Perilus!' bellowed Krysis. 'It's not fantastic at all. Hysteria is your sister! We can't leave the poor girl languishing in jail. Scorcha, why didn't YOU do anything?'

'I couldn't. Believe me, I've been thinking about nothing else ever since – how to get

Hysteria out. The guard's the problem. He's so dim he can't believe that I'm a man and she's a girl.' Scorcha looked thoroughly dejected. 'I'm very fond of Hysteria,' he added and blushed, rather fetchingly I thought.

'What? What did you say?' boomed Krysis. 'You're fond of my daughter?'

'I just meant, I meant, I meant I wouldn't want to see her come to any harm,' Scorcha hastily answered.

Krysis was pacing up and down like a sandal-less centurion on hot coals. 'It had better be nothing more than that, my boy,' he snapped at the charioteer. 'I've got much bigger plans for my daughter than marrying a former slave. I've fixed up a very important meeting with an old client, Pompus. He's looking for a wife and Hysteria would be perfect. Plus, it means a big marriage dowry will be paid – and we need the money.'

Flavia's face fell. 'Oh, darling. Do we have to? Hysteria is only fourteen.'

'And that's the age at which girls in Rome get married.' Krysis shrugged. 'What's the problem? We shall have one less mouth to feed AND we'll get a good dowry. I'm sure Pompus will like Hysteria.'

'Yes, darling,' agreed Flavia. 'But Hysteria is fourteen and Pompus is – what – fifty?'

'Fifty-seven,' Krysis corrected. 'Yes, it's a – it's a bit of an age gap.'

KRAAARRKKK! BIT OF AN AGE GAP! Tartan togas! Pompus was almost dead! Hysteria might as well marry a corpse! Krysis caught the look of horror on Flavia's face, not to mention poor Scorcha's. He looked crushed, as if a rhinoceros had just sat on him.

'We can't afford to be sentimental about this, Flavia. We have rent and food to pay for. How can I track down the Mint thief if I'm half dead from hunger?' Krysis asked.

'I'm making pizzas,' Flavia pointed out.

'Pizzas? Pizzas? I don't know what you're

talking about.' Krysis waved his hands dismissively. 'Pompus is coming to supper tonight and Hysteria MUST BE HERE.'

'*Ahem, ahem*,' I began and waited until I had everyone's full attention because I'd just thought up a cunning and stunningly awesome plan. 'I wonder if I might make a suggestion.'

'If you must,' Krysis muttered. 'Though I doubt it will make any difference.'

'Are we talkin' about the same Pompus who walked into the Temple of the Vestal Virgins last week because his eyesight is so poor, and he had to be rescued?'

'Yes, we are,' snapped Krysis.

'Then there's no problem,' I said evenly. 'Hysteria is here among us, right now. She's sittin' exactly THERE!' I pointed dramatically with one wing at Scorcha.

'*What?*' chorused Krysis, Flavia, Perilus and Scorcha.

'Look,' I continued (even more dramatically),

'Scorcha is still wearin' Hysteria's clothes. A little bit of make-up and he could easily pass for her. He can be presented to Pompus almost as he is. Pompus is half blind and won't be able to tell the difference.'

'Croakbag,' Flavia whispered in horror. 'You're mad.'

But Perilus was doubled up with laughter. In fact, he was rolling about on the floor, clutching his stomach.

Krysis simply stood there and allowed a huge smile to sweep across his face. 'That's brilliant! Just brilliant! Croakbag, you've saved the day.'

'Again,' I added, just for good measure.

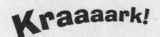

7. Ostriches CAN Fly!

Flavia was wobbling about like a headless chicken, fretting about Hysteria. 'What can we do? The dear girl shouldn't be in jail and Scorcha shouldn't be taking her place. It's ridiculous. Croakbag, can't we get her out before tonight?'

'I'm afraid not. The jail will be shut now. It's gone five o'clock. In any case, we have work to do. Krysis needs to get wine and nibbles for our esteemed guest and you've got a whole pile of cookin' to do before Pompus gets here. Fussia can help you. I have to see to the lovely, bashful Mysteria that's sittin' by the table and lookin' rather anxious.'

Do you like my new name for Hysteria? I think it's rather clever of me. It combines her real name with an element of mystery, do you see?

Whaddya mean, it's not all that clever? Did you think of it? NO! Who thought of it then? I did. Me. *Corvus you-know-whatticus.*

I did a couple of flaps with the old wing-things and landed on the table beside the charioteer.

'Cheer up,' I croaked.

'Croakbag, you've really landed me in hot soup. I can't pass as a girl! And I certainly can't be as beautiful and elegant as Hysteria.'

Perilus almost choked when he heard that. 'Elegant? Hysteria? She's about as elegant as a hippopotamus with a limp and a beard.'

'Darling, that isn't very nice,' murmured Flavia.

'Exactly,' grinned Perilus. 'That's what I mean.'

Flavia shook her head and sighed. 'Children,' she murmured. 'What can you do?'

'Sell them,' Krysis barked. 'I'm off to get the nibbles. Croakbag, you'd better get that young charioteer sorted.'

'Come on, Mysteria. Coochy-coochy-coo! Come with me!'

We went upstairs, with Scorcha dragging his feet as if he was off to the Colosseum to be fed to the lions or, worse, the giraffes. Why is that worse, I hear you ask? Because it takes so much longer! *Hurr hurr hurr hurr!* Raven joke. *Toc-toc-toc.*

I sat Scorcha down in Hysteria's little room. 'I am now goin' to turn you into a vision of beauty, just like Hysteria,' I told him. 'However, it may take a little while and I may have one or two problems on account of the fact that I don't have opposable thumbs. I do have opposable wings, but they're not quite as effective as fingers when it comes to applyin' the old face paint.'

Scorcha turned white. 'You're going to put Hysteria's make-up on me? But you're a raven.'

'I am indeed a raven. Well spotted. You can't do this yourself, Scorcha, whereas I've often seen Hysteria shovin' the old lipstick around her face, not to mention plasterin' her eyes with the black stuff, tryin' to make herself look like Queen Cleopatra. Now then, you just keep your face still and your mouth shut and let me get on with it.'

'But how am I going to make chit-chat with Pompus? He's bound to realize I'm a man.'

I took a step back and looked steadily at him. At least that was what I was going to do, but I was too close to the edge of the table and when I stepped back there wasn't any table left and I fell off. At least that put a smile on Scorcha's face.

The thing was, I knew Hysteria was in love with Scorcha and I was pretty sure that he liked her a lot too, so of course Scorcha wouldn't want Hysteria to get married to Pompus, would he? *Good point, Croakbag*, I thought to myself, so I clambered back on to the table and fixed Scorcha with a beady eye.

'Listen, we have to stop Hysteria bein' married off to Pompus. I think we're agreed on that, are we not?'

Scorcha leaped to his feet, eyes sparking like Vesuvius in mid-eruption. 'I will never, ever, EVER let that happen!' he declared.

'Good. Now sit down, please. Thank you. This evenin' your task is simple. Say as little as possible and behave like an idiot.'

'Why would I want to be an idiot?'

'Would Pompus want to marry an idiot? I don't think so. He'd be too worried that people would laugh at him.'

'What should I do, do you think?'

'Laugh at everythin'? A silly little baby laugh? Fall over? Spill things?'

'But Krysis will be so mad at me!' Scorcha protested. 'He'll be furious!'

'Scorcha!' I cried sternly. 'You are doin' this for Hysteria, to save her from a fate worse than death. In any case, everythin' will turn out fine.

It may take a year or three for Krysis to forgive you, but all will be well in the end. Now keep still and don't open your mouth.' And I picked up the lipstick in my beak and began.

Boy, did I have fun! Yes, I did! I must say it's quite difficult to apply make-up when you have to hold the lipstick in your beak. It does tend to slip about a bit, but by the time I'd finished I'd created a masterpiece. Scorcha picked up Hysteria's hand mirror and stared at himself in horror.

'I look like a monster from the depths of the sea,' he complained.

'Exactly. Or would you rather have Pompus fall in love with YOU?'

Hurr hurr hurr! That was quite enough for Scorcha. His shoulders slumped.

'Cheer up,' I told him. 'It will all be over soon and tomorrow you can climb into your chariot and show the world what a great charioteer you are.'

Just as I finished speaking there was a loud knock at the front door, such as it was. Pompus himself had arrived. The great man turned out to be rather short, rather tubby and rather bald. He reminded me of an ostrich egg, but with arms and legs. And a wig. Can you picture that? Probably not.

'When will I see the girl?' Pompus demanded. 'Why is she taking so long? She'd better not be wasting my time. I haven't got time to waste. My time is very important to me and cannot be wasted. Wasting time is something I abhor.'

Goodness, Pompus sounded rather – er –
pompous. And I must say he wasted an awful
lot of time telling us how much he hates time-
wasting. Listening to him blathering on made

me feel very glad that I don't have to marry anyone. Mind you, I did have a girlfriend once. She flew off with some other bonkers bird. Mad? He was absolutely ravin'! Oh, I crack myself up sometimes. **Kraaarrk!**

Whaddya mean, you think that's a rubbish joke? Can you do better? I doubt it. Anyhow, Pompus was still prattling on.

'I want to see your daughter, Krysis. She'd better not be ugly. I hate ugly people. Ugly people shouldn't be allowed to exist. They should be kept indoors, preferably somewhere dark. When I become Emperor, I shall ban ugly things. I'm badly affected by ugliness. I think I might be allergic to it. Urrrrgh! What's that dreadful black thing over there? A raven? You have a beastly, UGLY raven in your house? How can you put up with it? It's a PET? Urrrrgh! I think I need another drink.'

DID YOU HEAR WHAT HE SAID? ABOUT ME?! HE CALLED ME 'IT'! HE

THINKS I'M AN 'IT' AND I'M UGLY! I
can't believe it. Excuse me a moment while I
pull myself the right way up. I was so astonished
and HURT by what that man said I lost my grip
and ended up hanging upside down from my
perch. Very undignified. I've decided I don't like
Pompus and I sincerely hope that Krysis does not
marry poor Hysteria off to that BLIND, BALD,
BUMPTIOUS BIG-HEAD!

Just as Pompus was finishing
his little lecture on the
subject of ugliness,
who should come
down the stairs
but Hysteria, or
rather *My*steria,
accompanied by
her mother, and did
she look beautiful? Er, no.

Well, that's to say Flavia looked lovely of course, but Mysteria's make-up looked as if it had been put on with a soup ladle. Lipstick was smeared from ear to ear. There was so much black around her eyes that all you could see was a sort of dark, black cave and somewhere in that cave there were two eyes peeping out like a pair of curious bats.

Now who could possibly have done that to her face? I really couldn't say, *hurr hurr hurr!*

'Er, um, oooh,' hesitated Krysis, looking definitely dismayed. 'This is my wife, Flavia, and this is my daughter, Hysteria – I think. Is it? Is that you, Hysteria?'

Mysteria broke into squeals of laughter. 'Oh, Daddy! Of course it's me! And is this the man you were telling me about – Pimple?'

'Pompus!' growled Pompus, setting his wig straight and glaring furiously at Mysteria.

'Oh, Pomple, I'm so sorry!' giggled Mysteria.

'POM-PUS!' he roared.

'Shall we sit and eat?' suggested Flavia, sensibly

moving things on. 'Do come to the table. You're
most welcome here, Pompus.' She gave Mysteria
a quick glance and winked at her, I mean him.
Oh yes! Flavia knew what was going on!

Mysteria lay down on a couch and immediately
fell off. She kicked her feet in the air and laughed
until tears ran down her cheeks.

'Silly me. I'm always falling off my couch!'

'Hysteria, you have NEVER fallen off your
couch before,' Krysis snapped, beginning to
realize what Mysteria was up to. 'Get off that
floor at once!'

Mysteria gave Daddykins a silly smile and climbed back on to her couch. The table was already piled high with food. Everyone began to eat and all went quiet, but only for a short while. The main course was roast ostrich, carried in by Flippus Floppus. As he neared the table, he was so gobsmacked by the sight of Scorcha dressed as Hysteria and smothered in make-up that he tripped over her legs.

The tray went flying. The roast ostrich went flying. It landed squarely on Pompus's head, bounced off, skidded across the floor, taking Pompus's wig with it, and landed at my feet. So I ate it. (The ostrich of course, not the wig.)

Well, the others weren't going to, were they? Apart from the fact that it had been on the floor, they were all too busy shouting at each other and trying to breathe life back into Pompus.

He was also lying on the floor in a not much better state than the ostrich, which had knocked him unconscious.

Eventually, they managed to bring him round and Krysis and Flavia showered him with apologies. I don't know how many times they said sorry, but it was about seventy-two. Even Mysteria joined in, although she didn't mean it. I could see that smile lurking on her face, despite the wagonload of cosmetics I'd spread across it.

Pompus left in a fury, declaring Mysteria to be the ugliest, stupidest creature he had ever seen. But, although the evening had been a dreadful failure, it was also a great success, at least for Hysteria and Mysteria. And who made THAT happen? Me. Croakbag. *Corvus maximus intelligentissimussimus.* Go on, give us a biscuit!

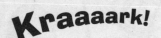

8. Who on Earth is Bob?

Big problems followed. As soon as Pompus had
stormed out of the house, Krysis turned on
Scorcha. He roared and raged like Vesuvius in
the *vomitorium*. Scorcha scraped away at his face,
trying to get all the make-up off and defend
himself at the same time.

'You thought it was a good idea for me to
pretend to be your daughter,' the charioteer
pointed out. 'Did I ask to be Hysteria? No, I
didn't. YOU asked me.'

'True.' I nodded wisely.

'It wasn't my idea either!' yelled Krysis. 'It was
that stupid bird's!'

And they both turned and looked at me. ME!
As if I was some sort of major criminal. Hadn't
I saved Hysteria? Hadn't I managed to put

Scorcha and Hysteria's little love affair back on track? Yes, I had. Did anyone say thank you? No, they did not. Huh. Well, just for once they can keep their bloomin' biscuits and I hope they choke on 'em. Get over it! Besides, there were more important matters to see to, such as getting Hysteria out of jail.

First thing the next morning, Flavia was making plans. She wrote a note that she was going to ask Perilus to take to the Imperial Prison.

Dear Numbskull Guard,
The person you call Scorcha is
in fact my daughter Hysteria.
She's fourteen and innocent.
Release her at once, you brainless
twaddle–head.

I suggested it might be an idea to leave out the numbskull and brainless twaddle-head bits. 'I don't think it'll put the guard in a very cooperative mood.'

Flavia crossed those bits out, called for Perilus and he set off, note in hand. Then she got on with pulling pizzas out of the oven as fast as she could. They'd been selling like hot – cakes? No, like hot pizzas! Ha ha, another raven joke and yes, I know, it's not very good.

My newly poor family desperately needed some dosh since Krysis had spent almost everything on rent and entertaining Pompus. Krysis himself had started working as a lowly clerk for an important lawyer. But there still wasn't enough money. What would they do without me to sort them out? Drop down dead probably. Let's hope that doesn't happen.

Meantime, Scorcha was needed at the Colosseum for the day's chariot race. If the Green Team wanted him to race, they'd have to pay him, so he should be OK as long as he didn't get shipwrecked. Shipwrecked – that's what we Romans call a major crash in a chariot race. Everyone leaps to their feet and yells, 'SHIPWRECK!'

Chariot racing is very dangerous. Sometimes chariots collide. Their wheels come off and go bouncing in all directions. SHIPWRECK! The driver is thrown to the ground. He has to cut himself free from the reins tied round his waist otherwise he'll be dragged to his death by the horses and get run over by who knows how many other chariots. Urgh! Makes me shudder to think about it, but the Romans love a shipwreck. It's a dangerous, exciting, life-or-death moment. Every time Scorcha gets into that chariot to race, he's taking his life in his hands. In other words, he's BRAVE. Give him a biscuit!

'But how am I going to get to the Colosseum without being spotted by Crabbus and Septicaemia?' Scorcha asked me.

Dear reader, please note that Scorcha ASKED ME. Did he ask Krysis or Perilus or even Trendia? No, he asked me, a raven. Why, you might ask? Because I am the most intelligent and creative creature around. *Corvus you-know-whatticus.* **Kraaarrk!**

And did I have a good idea? Of course I did. I had the perfect answer: I showed Scorcha the Time Machine that Maddasbananus had built.

He stared at it thoughtfully. 'It's on wheels,' he remarked. 'That's clever. Why is there an hourglass on top?'

'Don't ask. It's one of Maddasbananus's inventions.'

'Ah,' murmured Scorcha, understanding at once.

'You get inside,' I told the charioteer. 'I'll get Flippus Floppus and Maddasbananus to push you to the Colosseum. When they say it's all clear, you just walk out and Bob's your uncle.'

'I haven't got an uncle,' said Scorcha.

'It's just an expression,' I sighed.

'Oh, right. Sounds odd to me. What does it mean?'

'It means that, um –' I was stunned. I couldn't think how to explain it at all. Bob's your uncle? 'Listen, it's just somethin' you say when somethin' can be done easily. I have no idea why there's an Uncle Bob in it. The important thing is that we get you to the Colosseum without bein' seen by anyone.'

'Will Uncle Bob be in the Time Machine with me?' asked Scorcha, still puzzled.

'THERE IS NO UNCLE BOB! Look, can we forget about Uncle Bob, eh? Just get in there, shut the door and shut your mouth.'

Scorcha scrambled in and I slammed the door behind him. Toasted togas! Some people do go on about things. I mean, get over it!

I hurried off and grabbed Maddasbananus and Flippus. Between them they managed to push the wardrobe out of Trendia's house, only to come face to face with Septicaemia.

'Where are you off to with that cupboard?' she shouted.

'None of your business,' said Maddasbananus.

'Don't you talk to me like that, you young bit of muck.'

The inventor ignored her and carried on pushing.

'Oy! You've got an hourglass stuck on top of that cupboard! What's it doing up there? Are you stealing stuff? You are, aren't you? Oh yes, I know what you're like. You're thieves!'

I decided I would have to join in. 'Septicaemia, they're not thieves. Maddasbananus made this wardrobe and we're taking it to market to sell.'

'Who's going to buy a cupboard with a stupid egg timer on top?' snapped the old bag.

'Actually, it's a Time Machine, sort of,' Maddasbananus explained.

'Yeah!' I shouted. 'And it's time to go. Bye-eeee!'

Off we went, with me perching on top of the hourglass like some minor god in raven form.

We rolled all the way to the Colosseum. The noise was unbelievable. Thousands and thousands were shouting. I even heard some of them shouting for Scorcha. The Green Team were mighty pleased to see him, all except for Jellus.

'What are you doing here?' he demanded.

'I've come to race,' Scorcha told the captain.

'Tough. You're not racing. There isn't room in the team for you.'

The other members of the Green Team were aghast. 'But Scorcha's brilliant! He has to race. Besides, you're getting too fat and heavy to race, Jellus.'

'WHO'S THE CAPTAIN HERE!' roared Jellus.

'You are,' the team whispered, backing off.

Something had to be done, but what and by whom? My brain was on red alert, but I didn't need to do anything because Jellus suddenly noticed me.

'Aargh! A giant black bird! It's a bad omen. Get it out! Wring its neck!'

Jumping Jupiter! The man must be mad! *Wring its neck?* How very unkind and not at all polite. We hadn't even been introduced.

Jellus came thundering towards me, hands

outstretched and ready to do some wringing.
I flapped away from him and Flippus Floppus
rather helpfully stuck out one foot. Jellus tripped,
stumbled forward straight into a wooden post
and knocked himself out. **_BOOFF!_** Oh dear.
Such a shame. Now he wouldn't be able to racc.
Who could possibly take his place?

'Scorcha!' shouted one of the Green Team.
'Get yourself ready – the race starts in ten
minutes!'

Oh boy! Things were falling into place at
last, especially for Jellus, who certainly fell into
something. *Hurr hurr!* The race was on. The
chariots were all lined up. The horses were
pawing the dusty ground. The starter's flag
was raised. Get ready, Scorcha! Is he the best
charioteer ever? Yes, he is! Give the lad a biscuit!
Give the horses a biscuit! The race is on!

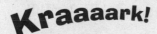

9. Maddasbananus to the Rescue!

It was a great race. The Reds held the lead right from the start, but Scorcha, riding for the Greens, was close behind. There just didn't seem to be an opportunity to overtake. The crowds were all shouting on their teams and the noise was like thunder, what with the pounding of hooves and screeching of racing wheels. Talk about excitement! I was leaping about myself, screaming so loudly I'm surprised my beak didn't come off.

Then, right at the last corner, Scorcha sneaked out to overtake and the Reds, still in front, moved out to stop him getting past.

With a sudden burst of speed from his frothing, slick-with-sweat horses, Scorcha dived down on the INSIDE! It was a stunning, brave move and it took the Reds by surprise. Scorcha slipped ahead and held his tiny lead right up to the winning post.

Scorcha had won. Hooray! The crowd went wild. Now they had a new hero. The crowd love it when someone young and new appears on the scene, especially someone like Scorcha. I think it's his lovely big smile. Something that birds find quite tricky. It's very difficult to twist a hard thing like a beak into a smile. You end up looking as if you've just flown into a brick wall.

Anyhow, Scorcha was the toast of Rome. People everywhere were talking about 'that fantastic new charioteer, Screecher' on the street. They meant Scorcha, but you know how people mispronounce things. That morning I heard him being called Screecher, Squeaker, Squawker, Scooter, Scawful, Stalker – everything except his proper name.

The only person who wasn't happy was Jellus, once he'd woken up from his unexpected morning nap. He was, after all, still captain of the Green Team and I could tell from the look on his face that he was deeply annoyed by Scorcha's success. It was the sort of face that spelled trouble.

Whaddya mean, faces can't spell anything? I know that! It's an expression, you diddle-brain. I bet you knew really. You were just trying to wind me up and yes, THAT'S an expression too.

Anyhow, meanwhile, thanks be to Jupiter, Hysteria was out of jail, but where was Perilus?

'He's in prison,' Hysteria told us. 'The guard wasn't very happy when he read your note, Mater. You called him a brainless twaddle-head and a numbskull. Well, the brainless, twaddle-headed, numbskull guard can't read so gave Perilus the letter to read out loud to him, but Perilus didn't know he wasn't supposed to say the crossed-out bits. Then the guard got angry and all miffed and began to cry. He said he wasn't going to help anyone who called him names. So Perilus said we should swop clothes and then I could escape dressed like him and he'd leave after me. We changed clothes and I walked out, but, when

Perilus tried to leave, the guard said he couldn't because he was Scorcha and was supposed to be in jail.'

Poor Flavia. She didn't know what was going on and when Krysis came home at lunchtime he threw several fits.

'I don't believe it! Every time someone goes to that wretched jail, they get arrested! Where's Fussia? FUSSIA! Go to the jail at once and tell them to release Perilus or I'll have the guards thrown into jail and see how they like it! I have to get back to tracking down the Mint thief. I'm not getting anywhere at the moment. Who hid the money in my room? It can't have been one of us. It can't have been a slave. Where would a slave get ten thousand silver *denarii* from? So who did it? And how?'

Yes, Krysis, I thought. *Indeed.* Personally speaking,, I was fairly sure WHO had done it. But I had no idea HOW and, until I knew that, I decided to keep my beak shut.

Flavia went straight back to making pizzas. Demand was growing all the time and she was rushed off her graceful little feet. Since Fussia had now gone off to try to rescue Perilus, she got Hysteria to help. Unfortunately, Hysteria spent most of her time staring out of the window in the hope of seeing Scorcha and she managed to burn a whole batch. They caught fire while Flavia was elsewhere. Hysteria became hysterical and threw the flaming pizzas out of the window. They went zooming across the yard and scored a direct hit on Septicaemia's endless load of washing which was hanging up to dry. The next thing Crabbus's best toga suddenly had a big, burnt hole right in the middle of it.

Crabbus and Septicaemia came hurtling
outside, waving their arms and yelling.
Septicaemia was clutching a broom and she
hastily beat out some of the flames. Crabbus tore
his toga from the washing line and held it up for
inspection.

'Look!' he yelled. 'Look what you've
done, you stupid, stupid girl! How
am I supposed to wear this?!'

He flung the toga round his shoulders and, as luck would have it, the big, burnt hole appeared right over his rather fat and bulgy bottom. So now Crabbus was yelling and bleating about his toga and Hysteria was in tears at the window.

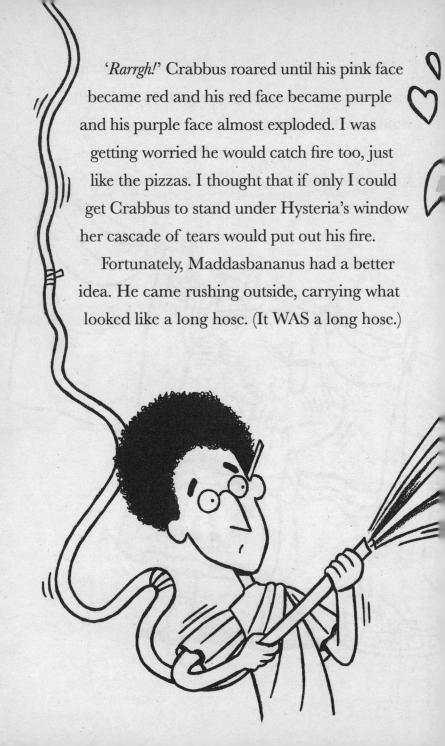

'*Rarrgh!*' Crabbus roared until his pink face became red and his red face became purple and his purple face almost exploded. I was getting worried he would catch fire too, just like the pizzas. I thought that if only I could get Crabbus to stand under Hysteria's window her cascade of tears would put out his fire.

Fortunately, Maddasbananus had a better idea. He came rushing outside, carrying what looked like a long hose. (It WAS a long hose.)

A sudden torrent of water gushed out and hit Crabbus full in the face, splashed past him and soaked Septicaemia as well. That shut them both up, but only for a few seconds.

Crabbus stood there, dripping wet, mouth open, wearing a toga with a hole over his bottom. Septicaemia, speechless with rage, was streaming with water and had wet hair plastered across her face. There was a moment of flabbergasted silence and then —

'*AAAAAAAAAARRRRRRGGGHHHH!* WHAT ARE YOU DOING?'

Maddasbananus grinned. 'It works! My new invention works!'

'What is it?' I asked politely, while Crabbus and Septicaemia continued their Dance of the Glowing Ghastlies.

'It's my Portable Fire Hose for the Home,' Maddasbananus declared proudly. 'By Jupiter, I think it's the first time one of my inventions has actually worked! My idea is that every house will have one of these and if there's a small fire it can easily be put out without having to call the Fire Brigade. It's going to make me millions!'

Crabbus's eyes were popping with anger. 'You idiot!' he growled. 'We could have drowned!'

'I was worried,' Maddasbananus explained. 'I thought you might have a fit and the hose was the best way to calm you down.'

'You should be pleased,' I told Crabbus. 'Maddasbananus saved you from havin' a fit.'

118

'Pleased?' roared Crabbus, who was now definitely having a raging fit. 'Look at me! Look at my toga! Look at my wife! I shall write to the magistrate about this, just you wait and see. You'll go to jail for this, both of you!'

I shook my shaggy, feathered head. 'Crabbus, my dear man, I think you'll find that ravens cannot be put in prison. Reason one: ravens are birds and birds don't go to jail. We fly free. Why, you might ask? Because, reason two, we have wings, *ergo*, we can fly and escape through the bars. Reason three: Roman law only applies to humans. *Ergo*, no jail for me. Reason four: the magistrate will no doubt think your noddle, that is to say, your head, is missin' somethin', namely a brain, and throw the case out and declare that you're wastin' his time.'

(*Ergo*, as you may remember, is Latin and it simply means 'therefore' or 'it follows that . . .'. Aren't you learning a lot? Yes, you are. Well done. Biscuits all round.)

119

Sadly, Crabbus wasn't prepared to learn anything.

'Think you're clever, don't you?' he snarled. 'Well, there's nothing to stop the magistrate putting HER in prison.' He pointed at Hysteria. 'Setting fire to togas is a punishable offence! So there! You can stick that in your beak! Ha!'

I didn't like to tell him that we'd only just got Hysteria *out* of jail. He wasn't supposed to know. Isn't life complicated? Yes, it is.

Anyhow, Crabbus went storming off with Septicaemia, with his bottom still showing through the hole in his toga. Stop sniggering – don't forget he was already wearing a toga when he tried on the holey one, so all you could see was more toga.

But at least Hysteria had stopped crying. This was probably because Scorcha had been safely delivered back from the chariot races in the Time Machine. What's more, he came back with Perilus, who had escaped from prison having changed places with Fussia, who was now in jail in his place. She hurried downstairs to greet him.

'Are you all right? You're so thin! I'll make you some food. You must be exhausted. Sit down. Lie down. Are you ill? How about your teeth? Are they all right? Did your hair fall out? You must feel filthy. Have a bath. I'll fetch some water. Wash behind your ears. Are your eyes dirty?'

Who knows how long Hysteria would've gone babbling on, but fortunately Krysis came striding in from outside. He looked pretty pleased with himself too.

'Our troubles will soon be over, I think,' he declared, smiling broadly at all of us.

'Really?' I croaked.

'I have solved the money problem, but really it's all because of you, Hysteria.'

'Me?' she squeaked. 'But I haven't done anything, Pater. I mean, yes, I had a teeny, tiny, ipsy-wipsy accident with some flaming pizzas, but it really wasn't my fault, and if Septicaemia hadn't been stupid enough to hang Crabbus's toga on the washing line then his bottom wouldn't be –'

'Hysteria, be quiet!' snapped Krysis. 'I haven't got a clue what you're talking about. All you have to do is dress well for this evening and don't let that wretched raven anywhere near your make-up. I have found a husband for you and he's going to pay oodles of dosh to marry you! There! Isn't that fantastic?'

Hysteria simply gawped at Pater.

Wretched raven or not, I wanted to know who the lucky man was, so I asked.

Krysis did his impression of a sunbeam again. 'Why, it's Fibbus Biggus!' he said and Hysteria promptly fainted.

Nice one!' Perilus said, admiringly.

Well, at least Hysteria didn't burst into tears.

Give her a biscuit! **Kraaaark!**

10. Hmmmrrphlnnqrrgrrrrmph

A new day dawns and has much changed? Not really. In fact, if it's not one thing, it's another. I refer, of course, to the one thing – namely Hysteria getting married to Fibbus Biggus – and the other thing, that is Fussia still in prison, Scorcha still on the run, Crabbus still trying to get us all into jail and, oh dear, what's this coming down the street towards us? Why, it's young Perilus, my feisty pal, and he's got an elephant with him.

KRAAARRRK?? AN ELEPHANT?

Indeed. A fully grown African elephant, and Perilus is feeding it bits of pizza.

Whaddya mean? Elephants eat grass and leaves, not pizza! Were you there? No, you were not. So please close that toothy orifice in your face and keep it closed.

Elephants. Amazing creatures. One of my favourites. Blue whales. That's another favourite, and giraffes. Extraordinary. I must say that there are a whole pile of beasties that worry me. I mean, what is the point of a flea? Nasty little things. You can hardly even see them. But elephants – now they are MAJESTIC beasts.

This one was female and she told me she was called Hmmmrrphlnnqrrgrrrrmph, though I may not have spelled her name correctly. She wasn't at all sure about the spelling herself. Elephants are good at doing all sorts of things – humming, for example; they love to hum – but they're hopeless at spelling. It's a well-known fact. You ask an elephant to spell anything you like, even something easy like 'cat', and all they do is shuffle their feet and blink at you because they're embarrassed.

Sadly, Hmmmrrphlnnqrrgrrrrmph was the

only one who could actually say her name so
I told her I'd call her Tiddles, which made her
laugh so much she wet herself, and then said she
was definitely a tiddler of some sort.

Of course, I said all this in elephant language,
which is basically animal language, so Perilus and
everyone else simply stood and stared at us while
we had this rather civilized conversation. Krysis
wasn't at all pleased when Tiddles laughed so
much and had her little accident, mostly over his
left foot. He hopped about a bit and scowled and

shook his foot, but he didn't say anything because you don't, do you? Not when the culprit is several metres taller than you are, not to mention several metres wider and several tonnes heavier.

Then Tiddles startled everyone by curling her trunk round Perilus and popping him on to her back.

'Put him down!' cried Flavia. 'He'll fall!'

'No, I won't,' said Perilus and he stood up on one leg and began hopping along Tiddles's back.

It was Krysis who asked the most important question. (Paters and maters do tend to do that. It's obsessive-compulsive behaviour if you ask me.)

'Why?' Krysis shouted up at Perilus. 'Why have you brought an elephant here?'

'I didn't. I was out walking and I saw this elephant standing by the side of the road and gave her a bit of Mater's pizza I had left over and she followed me home. I told her to go away, but she wouldn't leave me alone. Anyway, she's cute.'

'You can't keep her.' Krysis folded his arms and stuck his jaw out, just like Perilus had done earlier.

'*I* didn't ask to keep *her*,' Perilus pointed out. 'I think *she* wants to keep *me*.'

Flavia linkcd an arm with her husband. 'I'm not sure how you can make an elephant go away,' she murmured.

Krysis perked up. He'd had an idea. 'Maybe we can sell her.'

'Just like me?' Hysteria suddenly blurted angrily. 'You like selling things, don't you, Pater? You want to sell me to Fibbus Biggus and now you want to sell the elephant. Don't you ever think of how we might FEEL about that?'

Krysis turned a delicate shade of pink. 'I didn't mean – I mean, it's just that – it's not as simple as that, Hysteria. We have very little money and I'm trying to look after everyone. It's a hard life when you have no money.'

'So you want to sell your daughter?' Hysteria

repeated hotly. 'And an elephant that isn't even yours?'

'It's not selling,' Krysis said weakly. 'It's marriage. You'll be his wife.'

'But Fibbus Biggus will give you money and you'll give me to him. That's selling, Pater. Fibbus will buy me as if I'm just a bag of apples.'

I coughed loudly, several times. I was trying not to laugh at the idea of Hysteria as a bag of apples. In any case, a little idea was growing in my feathery brain. I am not called *Corvus brainus mega-superbus-and-brilliantissimus* for nothing. There are times when my brain lights up like Nero's Rome when it caught fire and burnt to the ground.

'Excuse me,' I began. '*Ahem, ahem.*' (That's me clearing my throat again.) 'If I might just interject at this point. Rather than sell Tiddles –'

'Tiddles?' everyone chorused, even Perilus.

'Indeed. Tiddles is the elephant's name.'

'Highly appropriate,' Krysis muttered VERY

sarcastically. He gave his foot a last shake. I
pretended to ignore him.

'*Ahem.* Rather than sell Tiddles, why don't we
make use of her? Here we have a strong and
powerful creature. If we look after her, we can
maybe get her to help us. Have you seen the
great new buildin's the Emperor Tyrannus has
started on? When I've been flyin' over our great
city, I've sometimes seen elephants workin' on
the buildin' sites. They pull heavy loads. They
lift things that a man can't lift. We could hire out
Tiddles. The construction
workers will pay good money
for a tame elephant.'

'How do we know she's
tame?' grunted Krysis.

I pointed at Tiddles
with one wing.
Perilus was doing a
handstand on top of
her head.

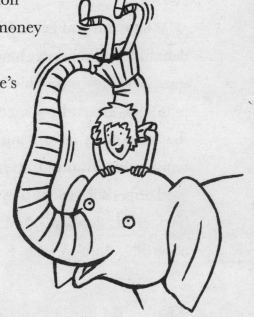

'How much tamer than that do you want her to be?' I asked.

Krysis stroked his chin. Maybe he thought it would help make it stick out even further. It didn't. 'You might have a point, Croakbag. Just this once, you might have a point. But where can we keep an elephant?'

At that moment, Crabbus and Septicaemia burst out of their apartment, having realized that there was an elephant outside their front door.

'You can't park that elephant there!' yelled Crabbus.

'Where did you get it from?' Septicaemia demanded. 'You don't have any money. You must have stolen it. Thief! Thief! Arrest that man! No, arrest those men! No, I mean arrest that man and that woman and that boy doing handstands. Handstands are NOT allowed in the yard, especially when they're being done on the back of an elephant! And arrest the elephant as well!'

Ye gods! (And I mean all of them: Jupiter, Neptune, Venus, Diana, Mars *et cetera*.) Anyhow, ye gods! That woman knew how to talk nonsense and make a fuss over nothing. Though, come to think of it, I had to admit an elephant was a bit more than 'nothing'.

All the noise brought Trendia and Maddasbananus outside. The inventor was standing on a strange contraption he had created. It was a plank of wood with wheels underneath it and as he trundled across the yard, desperately trying to balance, he fell off at least five times.

'What a beautiful creature!' declared Trendia, stroking Tiddles's trunk.

'Not as lovely as you,' Maddasbananus blurted out before turning bright red and falling off his plank again. 'Ow!' He clutched at his knee.

'Oh, Maddas!' Trendia put both hands to her flaming cheeks and gave the inventor a charming smile. Hmmmm. She dashed across to her fallen hero. 'You've scraped your knee. It's bleeding. Here, let me.' Trendia dabbed at Maddasbananus's knee with the hem of her dress. 'There.'

They looked into each other's eyes and *KAPOW!* Two hearts came fluttering out of their eyes and became entwined. At last! Hooray for Jupiter, King of the Gods, and hooray for Venus, Goddess of Love and Beauty. Ah! How sweet!

Whaddya mean, you feel sick? Don't be so pathetic. True love is a wonderful thing, as you will one day find out for yourself if you're lucky. Oh, so now you *are* being sick. Honestly, humans! Huh!

However, we mustn't spend too much time swimming in the warm and welcoming waters of the Pool of Lurve because The Ghastlies are still elephanting on about the elephant.

I think Tiddles understood most of what they were saying because she started stamping her feet and going in reverse.

'STOP!' yelled Crabbus. 'You daft beast!
You're backing into our house!'

SKRRRRUNK! SKRRRURRKKKK!!
KERRRASHHHHH!

The whole front porch began to lurch
to one side before gently tipping right
over and crashing to the ground,
scattering broken roof tiles
and pots far across
the yard.

'YOU IDIOT CREATURE!' bellowed Crabbus. And he and Septicaemia both started to kick at one of Tiddles's back legs. 'YOU (kick) STUPID (kick) STUPID (kick) PACHYDERM!'

Goodness me! Fancy someone like Crabbus knowing that other name for an elephant. You knew it too? You did? Well done. Bright lad! Or lass! Have a biscuit.

Good thing Tiddles was thick-skinned. Even so, she wasn't best pleased to find two angry midgets kicking her back leg, so she swivelled about, curled her trunk round the pair of them, lifted them high into the air, turned them upside down and gave them a good shake while blowing her trumpety trunk.

BLAAARRRR!

Septicaemia and Crabbus could only scream and yell as they were shaken so hard their clothing fell over their heads and all we could see was their underwear and two pairs of legs waggling about, which was quite a sight, I can tell

you. I've never seen such knobbly, hairy knees.
And that went for both of them!

Tiddles carefully put the pair back on the
ground, where they lay gasping and grunting as
they tried to catch their breath. At last Crabbus
regained the power of speech.

'You're ALL going to jail for this!' he screamed.
'The whole lot of you!'

11. A Word in the Emperor's Ear

Hmmmm. (That's me thinking.) Tiddles. Bit of a problem. It was all very well having an elephant around the place, but where were we going to keep her? Perilus hastily led Tiddles on to the road, away from the fuming Ghastlies.

I took to the air and flapped about a bit, searching for somewhere to put the beast. While I flapped, my brain was teeming, boiling over with all the problems that needed to be solved. Scorcha, for example. We couldn't hide him in the Time Machine forever and he had another big race coming up. Nor could we leave Fussia in prison forever. Then there was Hysteria and possible marriage to Fibbus Biggus. And The Ghastlies! They were bound to follow up their threat of jail. Problems, problems.

I soon spotted a small field and wood behind the house. That would have to do for now. 'Take Tiddles round to that field behind us,' I told Perilus. 'She can wander in the woods. And now I must disappear for a short while,' I added.

'Where?'

'Business, dear boy, business. Nothin' you need to know about.'

There are things to say to people and other things to keep quiet about. I, of course, am very clever and know exactly which is which.

Whaddya mean, I'm just a show-off big-head? Can you count to a hundred? You can? Oh well, you are human after all. You *are* human, aren't you? Good. Then please understand that counting to a hundred is considered pretty big stuff when you're an animal of any sort. Even centipedes can't count to a hundred and they've got more legs than you can shake a stick at. That's a strange expression, isn't it? I mean, why would you want to shake a stick at a centipede's legs anyway?

But I was off again, soaring through the skies of Rome before swooping down to the Emperor's palace, flitting through the odd window here and there before I eventually found Tyrannus himself, taking a bath.

'*Salve*, Tyrannus,' I croaked.

'Don't you ever knock? Do you have to come barging into my private bathroom?' the Emperor demanded, rather rudely I thought.

'When I have somethin' important to tell you, yes,' I remarked, casually preening my left wing.

'You've dumped a feather in the bath.' Tyrannus pushed it away with a big toe – an enormous toe. I'd never seen such a big big toe. 'What do you want?'

'Want?' I repeated. 'I want nothin'.'

'Then why come bothering me?'

'I have some information you might wish to put to good use.' I began preening my right wing. Tyrannus pushed at a couple more

feathers. He really did have the most enormous
big toes. I was fascinated by them.

'Do you mind not shoving your feathers in my
bath?'

'Pardon me. Bit tetchy this mornin'? Did you
get out of bed the wrong side?'

'If you must know, I *fell* out of bed. I had a bad
dream.' The Emperor sighed and closed his eyes.

'Well, I have some news that might cheer you up. Are you goin' to the chariot races this afternoon?' I started cleaning my tail feathers.

'Naturally. My public expect me to be there.' The Emperor suddenly changed the subject. 'How's Krysis?'

I lifted my head and looked straight at Tyrannus. 'Desperate. What do you expect?'

The Emperor shook his head. 'I don't have any choice, Croakbag. He's the only suspect I have so far. I suggest you get on with the investigation.'

'We've been busy. Neighbours, elephants, people poppin' in and out of jail. It takes up one's time. Krysis is doin' his best, but there are no real clues so far.'

Tyrannus lay back and sighed. 'So, you rascal, tell me your other news.'

'The races this afternoon,' I squawked. 'Watch Scorcha, in the Green Team. Put your money on him to win.'

Tyrannus nodded. 'I shall. And if he wins,

what then? No doubt you have a favour to ask in exchange for this information.'

'Scratch my back and I'll scratch yours. *Toc-toc-toc!*' I bobbed my head at him. 'Scorcha is meant to be in jail − a very small crime. He annoyed a neighbour.'

'If he's meant to be in jail, why isn't he?'

I thought of how Hysteria had changed places with Scorcha and Perilus had swopped places with his sister and Fussia had changed with Perilus and so on. 'It's a long story,' I told Tyrannus. 'I'll fill you in another time. If Scorcha wins, I'd like you to pardon him so that he can carry on winnin' races and you can carry on winnin' money because of it.'

Tyrannus shrugged. 'Consider it done. *Vale*, Croakbag.'

'*Vale*, Tyrannus.'

As I flew away from the palace, I smiled. Once Scorcha was pardoned, the prison guards would have to let Fussia go because, being rather short

of brainpower, they
probably still thought Fussia
was Scorcha. I reckoned I'd just
about solved that problem at least.

What was next? I was pondering on this when,
coming in to land back at the house, I was just
in time to see Maddasbananus and Perilus, back
from elephant duties, pushing the Time Machine
up the road. Obviously, Scorcha was on his way
to the Colosseum for his next big race. Putuponn,
The Ghastlies' little slave, was hanging out their
washing again and Hysteria was climbing out of
a back window. Eh? Very interesting. What was
she up to?

I settled in a nearby tree and watched as
Hysteria lowered herself to the ground, skulked
round the side of the house, joined the road a
bit further up and hurried after the disappearing
Time Machine. Aha! Of course! She was going

to the Colosseum too, to see
Scorcha race. Ah, young love!
Isn't it charming?

There was a rather burnt smell in the
air so I flew over to take a peek.
Flavia was making her pizzas
to take to the Colosseum, but
she was also getting into a bit
of a tizz, racing round the tiny kitchen and trying
to bake in the smallest oven in Rome, with only
Flippus Floppus to help her.

Poor Flippus. He really wasn't built for making
and baking. He kept tripping himself up and
a bit of raw pizza would go slapping
across the room. Or he'd spill bowlfuls
of pizza topping. The kitchen floor
was littered with squashed vegetables and
slices of sausage, making it so slippery that Flavia
herself was having trouble walking, and this was
the woman who normally glided about the place
as if she was on little wheels.

'It's ridiculous!' she cried. 'I should've made dozens of pizzas by now, but I've only managed to bake ten. Why isn't Fussia here to help?!'

'Still in jail,' I pointed out.

Flavia shot me a look of utter despair, opened her mouth wide, pulled at her hair and SCREAMED!

'*EEEEEEEEEAAAAAAHHHHHHHH!*'

Then she went completely crazy. She began picking up pots and pans and throwing them all over the place. Soon most of the kitchen wasn't a kitchen any more. It was bits of broken pottery all over the walls.

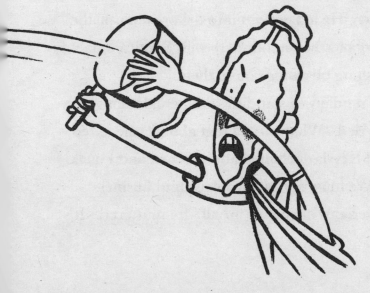

Krysis came racing in to see what all the noise was about. He just managed to duck in time as a large clay pot, half full of oil, went whizzing past his head and smashed against the wall behind him. Oil splattered out and dribbled down. Krysis hurried across to his shrieking wife and wrapped his arms round her so she couldn't move. At once she collapsed, sobbing, in his arms.

'I can't go on like this,' Flavia choked. 'It's impossible. This place, it's so small. The pizzas, Fussia in jail – I just can't do it any more.'

Krysis spoke to her quietly until she calmed down. He led her out into the open air of the yard and they stood there with Septicaemia's washing billowing round them.

Trendia was standing out there, looking very worried. 'What was all that about?' she asked, and Krysis explained about Flavia and Fussia.

'We must get this whole stupid business sorted out once and for all,' he muttered. 'It's ridiculous. Those prison guards are worse than useless. Sometimes I think it would be better if Scorcha had stayed in jail. Come on, we're going to go to the prison and demand Fussia's release. We'll prove she isn't Scorcha. Stupid, idiotic guards! Are they blind? Come on! You come too, Flippus, and Hysteria and Perilus. We'll all go. Hysteria!' shouted Krysis. 'Perilus! Where are they? Croakbag, you must know. Why aren't they answering?'

'Um, Perilus has gone to make sure Tiddles is all right and I think Hysteria went with him. She's not in the house.' I thought it best not to let on that Hysteria had gone off to watch Scorcha. Pater would NOT be happy about that!

'Wait,' said Trendia. 'Let me get my *stola*. I'm coming too.'

Krysis grunted. 'Thank you. That makes four of us. That should be enough. Come on!' And they set off for the prison.

Off they went, left, right, left, right, jaws jutting out. What a brave bunch they were, marching up the street. Give 'em all a biscuit.
Krraaarrk!

12. The Imperial Guard Strikes Back!

Of course, I had to go after them. I wanted to see all the action. Actually, I'd had to choose between going to the Colosseum to see Scorcha whizzing round the track at death-defying speed or sticking with Krysis and his gang and going to the prison. Decisions, decisions. I consulted my gut, that is to say my instincts, and they told me to keep an eye on Krysis.

By the time he reached the Imperial Prison, Krysis had really worked himself up into a state of high indignation. He went marching up to the two guards and Flavia, Trendia and Flippus Floppus closed in behind him.

'Release Fussia at once!' Krysis ordered.

'Why?' asked the Chief Guard, Plausible,

while guard number two, Ludicrus, yawned loudly.

'Because she has been wrongfully imprisoned.'

'Not so,' said Ludicrus. 'Firstly, there is no "she" in this prison at the moment and, secondly, we don't have anyone called Fussia.'

Krysis's eyebrows were tying knots in each other he was so angry. 'That's because you think she's the prisoner Scorcha.'

'Exactly!' snapped Plausible. 'She IS the prisoner Scorcha. That's why she's in prison. Because she's the prisoner!'

Then it was Flavia's turn. She tried her charm, fluttered her eyelashes, smiled and stroked Ludicrus's arm. 'The thing is,' she said lightly, 'there's been a mistake. Fussia is our slave. She came to the prison and swopped clothes with Perilus, who had swopped clothes with Hysteria,

who had swopped clothes with
Scorcha, who escaped, dressed
as a woman. Unfortunately,
you wouldn't let Fussia out
again because she was wearing
Scorcha's clothes and now you
think she actually is Scorcha.
But she isn't. She's Fussia.'

'Sorry?' said Ludicrus. 'Could you repeat that, please?'

Flavia did, but the guards still didn't quite understand it.

'So Scorcha is your slave –' began Plausible and Flavia shook her head and tried to keep smiling.

'No. Fussia is my slave.'

'OK. Fussia is your slave. She came to the prison and she swopped clothes with the prisoner?'

'Yes. Sort of. There are bits missing, but yes. There was some swopping going on. Quite a lot actually.' Flavia gave a little giggle, but the guard didn't think anything was funny at all.

Ludicrus pursed his lips. 'Are you saying your slave likes to dress as a man?'

Flavia sighed. 'No. I'm not saying that at all.'

'So why did she?'

'Why did she what?'

'Dress as a man.'

'She didn't – at least, only when she dressed as Scorcha.'

'Scorcha's a man,' declared Plausible and he turned to his pal. 'Scorcha's a man, isn't he? What have we got in prison? A man or a woman?'

'A man,' said Ludicrus. 'So that must be –'

'SCORCHA!' the two guards agreed.

'SCORCHA!' yelled the nearby crowd at the Colosseum, just like an echo. I smiled to myself. He must have won his race. Tyrannus owed me for that and Hysteria was probably going – hysterical! (But in a nice, admiring kind of way.)

Krysis stepped forward. 'Now listen here, you diddle-brained pair of nincompoops! That prisoner you think is Scorcha is our slave, Fussia. You'd better make sure she's released immediately or I'll, I'll –'

Krysis broke off, not sure what he'd do. In any case, the two guards were drawing themselves up to their full height and looking at Krysis very severely. This was not going to turn out well. I wanted to cover my eyes with my wing, but then I wouldn't be able to tell you what happened next.

'Right,' said Ludicrus. 'That's quite enough of your insults, calling us nincompoops. I don't even know what a nincompoop is, do you?' he asked his chief.

'I don't either, but it's certainly not Latin,' said Plausible. They both began to lower their spears in a rather pointed and threatening manner.

Plausible loomed over Krysis. 'I hereby arrest ALL of you for insulting the Imperial Guard in a language we don't even know and for assisting a slave in helping a prisoner escape.'

'And for dressing men as women and women as men,' added Ludicrus. 'Go on, get inside that prison and don't you dare start swopping clothes with ANYONE or I'll confiscate all of them! UNDERSTAND?! We've had quite enough of that sort of thing going on here recently. Go on, get moving!'

Trendia smiled at Plausible. 'Um, could I just say that I'm not really with them? I'm not family. I just came along to give them moral support.'

Plausible sneered. 'Moral support?' He turned to his companion. 'Have you ever heard the like? Moral support? What in the name of Jupiter is that?'

'No idea,' grunted Ludicrus and he poked Trendia with his spear. 'Go on, in you go.'

I perched on the wall by the prison and

watched my family (and Trendia) disappear inside. Oh dear. Everything was back to square one. Krysis was locked up again, only this time he had Fussia, Flavia, Flippus Floppus AND Trendia with him. Tortured togas! How on earth was I supposed to sort this lot out?

Watch out for the third and final part of
ROMANS ON THE RAMPAGE! Will Scorcha
win the Charioteer of the Year Award?

Will Perilus end up being squashed by Tiddles?

Will Fibbus Biggus marry Hysteria?

Will there be many more 'wills'? Plus –
WHO *DID* STEAL THE MONEY FROM
THE MINT?

PRAISE FOR
ROMANS ON THE RAMPAGE

'I like Perilus because he did dangerous things. I have noticed that Perilus is a bit like my brother because he always gets up to no good' – Katie Ryan

'I think it is actually the best book I ever read' – Menaal Fayyaz

'I can't wait for your next book' – Adam

'I think your books are amazing because you make them sound funny. You're the best author, do you think so too?' – Amy Drake

'Your book was really entertaining, and it made me laugh a lot. I hope you write another book like this one!' – Brooke

'I was reading the book at school and it was AMAZING' – Ronnie

'Thank you for writing Romans on the Rampage – it was a fantastic book. My favourite part was when Perilus and Scorcha were riding the goats and crashed' – Ellie-May

'I especially liked the part when Perilus fell off the washing line. It reminds me of when I fell off a log into a stinky river' – James Staniford

Ask Jeremy

Of all the books you have written, which one is your favourite?

I loved writing both **KRAZY KOW SAVES THE WORLD – WELL, ALMOST** and **STUFF**, my first book for teenagers. Both these made me laugh out loud while I was writing and I was pleased with the overall result in each case. I also love writing the stories about Nicholas and his daft family – **MY DAD**, **MY MUM**, **MY BROTHER** and so on.

If you couldn't be a writer what would you be?

Well, I'd be pretty fed up for a start, because writing was the one thing I knew I wanted to do from the age of nine onward. But if I DID have to do something else, I would love to be either an accomplished pianist or an artist of some sort. Music and art have played a big part in my whole life and I would love to be involved in them in some way.

What's the best thing about writing stories?

Oh dear – so many things to say here! Getting paid for making things up is pretty high on the list! It's also something you do on your own, inside your own head – nobody can interfere with that. The only boss you have is yourself. And you are creating something that nobody else has made before you. I also love making my readers laugh and want to read more and more.

Did you ever have a nightmare teacher?
(And who was your best ever?)

My nightmare at primary school was Mrs Chappell, long since dead. I knew her secret – she was not actually human. She was a Tyrannosaurus rex in disguise. She taught me for two years when I was in Y5 and Y6, and we didn't like each other at all. My best ever was when I was in Y3 and Y4. Her name was Miss Cox, and she was the one who first encouraged me to write stories. She was brilliant. Sadly, she is long dead too.

When you were a kid you used to play kiss-chase. Did you always do the chasing or did anyone ever chase you?!

I usually did the chasing, but when I got chased, I didn't bother to run very fast! Maybe I shouldn't admit to that! We didn't play kiss-chase at school – it was usually played during holidays. If we had tried playing it at school we would have been in serious trouble. Mind you, I seemed to spend most of my time in trouble of one sort or another, so maybe it wouldn't have mattered that much.

LAUGH YOUR Socks off with Jeremy STRONG

Jeremy Strong has written SO many books to make you laugh your socks right off. There are the Streaker books and the Famous Bottom books and the Pyjamas books and . . . PHEW!

Welcome to the JEREMY STRONG FAMILY TREE, which shows you all of Jeremy's brilliant books in one easy-to-follow-while-laughing-your-socks-off way!

MY BROTHER'S FAMOUS BOTTOM

Nicholas's baby brother, Cheese, is famous. Well, his bottom is, because he advertises Dumper disposable nappies . . .

THE HUNDRED-MILE-AN-HOUR DOG
Streaker is no ordinary dog; she's a rocket on four legs with a woof attached . . .

COSMIC PYJAMAS
Pyjamas are just pyjamas, right? Not when they're COSMIC PYJAMAS, swooooosh! . . .

COWS, CARTOONS, ELEPHANTS AND . . . ORANG-UTANS?!
Warning – may induce red cheeks and tears of laughter!

Jeremy Strong once worked in a bakery, putting the jam into three thousand doughnuts every night. Now he puts the jam in stories instead, which he finds much more exciting. At the age of three, he fell out of a first-floor bedroom window and landed on his head. His mother says that this damaged him for the rest of his life and refuses to take any responsibility. He loves writing stories because he says it is 'the only time you alone have complete control and can make anything happen'. His ambition is to make you laugh (or at least snuffle). Jeremy Strong lives near Bath with his wife, Gillie, three cats and a flying cow.

www.jeremystrong.co.uk